AN INSTANT CONNECTION

INSTA-SPARK #3

MELANIE MORELAND

MORELAND BOOKS, INC

An Instant Connection by Melanie Moreland

Registration # 1155685
ebook ISBN # 978-1-988610-18-4
Print ISBN # 978-1-988610-24-5

Edited and Proofed by
D. Beck
Lisa Hollett—Silently Correcting Your Grammar

Created with Vellum

DEDICATION

For Matthew who always puts me first

FOREWORD

This story was originally produced as a podcast on Read Me Romance. The ebook version contains extended content not found in the original narration.

Thank you to Alexa Riley and Tessa Bailey for inviting me to write a story for their subscribers. Check out Read Me Romance on Spotify, iTunes, Stitcher and Google Play.

CHAPTER ONE

MANDY

The cool, fall air hit me as I exited the tall Toronto skyscraper in the early evening. I breathed in deeply, ignoring the scent of exhaust fumes and the hundreds of people bustling past me, no doubt as anxious to be home as I was at the moment. I needed to get the smell of the stale, building air out of my lungs.

At least I was out of the office and away from my tyrant of a boss. Plus, it was Friday, which meant I had the whole weekend ahead of me. With a heavy sigh, I turned and headed toward the bus station a few blocks away.

Michelle had been on a tear today, worse than usual. HR had confirmed the hire of a new associate at the architectural company I worked for, and he was due to arrive on Monday. Michelle was the head administrative manager of the office, and she ran her department with an iron fist. When she found out a new person would be arriving and his office needed to be ready, she had snagged me and another woman from the temp pool and put us to work. Betty had "fallen ill" by noon, which left me on my own with Michelle, who simply could not be pleased today. It was rare she could be, and it seemed the new hire, Mr. Mackenzie, was particular and liked things a certain way.

The pictures of his work I helped unpack showed his creative, edgy style. His initials on each piece were a bold MM slashed in the corner in thick black ink. There was a box I emptied, under her watchful eye, filled with unique items from around the world. I had set them carefully on the shelves that lined the wall, knowing Mr. Mackenzie would probably move them to a different spot, but thankfully, they were unpacked. Obviously, the man had traveled extensively throughout his career. The way Michelle kept nattering on about him and how lucky the company was to have hired him, I assumed he was well known and admired. He had to be for her to pay that much attention to his office. I was sure the two of them would get along famously the way she was fussing.

When I first started at the company, I had looked forward to learning from Michelle, but once I began to work under her, I changed my mind. She was catty and unpleasant, only polite to her bosses and the managers she catered to daily. To her underlings, she was dismissive, curt, and at times, cutting. I kept my head down, did my work, and unobtrusively sent out as many resumes as I could.

I reached the bus stop, knowing I had already missed the seven o'clock bus, and would have to wait for the next one, which wasn't for forty-five minutes. It wasn't a bad place to wait—lots of benches situated around the large area, and it was well lit. Since it was one of the main stops, and most of the city buses came through, it was usually bustling; although, being later on a Friday night, it was fairly quiet.

A woman brushed past me, calling an apology over her shoulder as she rushed for a bus ahead of us that was beginning to close the doors. She waved frantically at the driver, her stuffed messenger bag bouncing off her back as she ran. I noticed how tired she looked as she met my gaze quickly, and without thinking, I lifted my hand to my mouth and whistled.

I was a great whistler, and the sound cut through the night. The driver hesitated, saw the woman, and waited. With a wave, she climbed on the bus, and I fist bumped the air.

"My good deed for the day," I muttered, made my way over to the bench, and sat down. I bent low, rubbing my calves. I hated high heels, but it was part of the "look" Michelle demanded of all the assistants in the office. I wore the lowest ones I could get away with, so I didn't face her wrath, but still, by the end of the day, my legs were always sore. All I wanted was to get home, kick off my heels, pour a large glass of wine, and have a soak in the tub.

"That is an impressive set of lips."

Startled, I looked up, meeting the eyes of a man. He was leaning against the streetlamp, his arms crossed. A bright, coppery mass of curls gleamed under the light. He was tall, his shoulders wide and thick, his coat stretched tight across his torso. He was near enough I could see the color of his eyes. Piercing, brilliant blue irises were set into a face I could only describe as gorgeous. He had high cheekbones and a strong jaw covered with more copper. His smile was lazy, his lips drawn back, showing off straight, white teeth, one corner of his mouth lifted higher than the other one, giving him a rakish air.

"I beg your pardon?"

"Great whistle."

"I was trying to get the attention of the bus driver."

"You got more than that. You got *my* attention."

I rolled my eyes, turning slightly on the bench. I was too tired to fend off a flirt—even one as handsome as him.

From the corner of my eye, I saw him step closer. "Do you know her?"

I sighed and faced him. I hated to be impolite—even to pushy strangers who couldn't take a hint. "Pardon me?"

"The woman you helped to make sure she caught her bus. Do you know her?"

"No."

He rubbed his jaw, seemingly reflective. I tried to ignore his hands, but I couldn't. I had a thing for hands, and his were incredible.

Large, with long, thick fingers that were still elegant, but looked as if they were capable of ripping a phone book in half with ease or caressing my skin with the softest of touches.

I blinked.

Where the hell did that thought come from?

I dug into my purse, searching for my earbuds.

"Do you often help strangers?"

I glanced up, surprised to see the man standing directly in front of me. Close up, he was even better looking. His wild hair hung low on his brow, and his eyebrows were darker, setting off his exceptional blue eyes. There were laugh lines around them, and from the impish grin he sported, I had a feeling he laughed a lot. As if he knew what I was thinking, his grin widened, two deep dimples popping in his cheeks, changing him from attractive to devastatingly handsome.

I blinked again.

What was his question?

"Oh, erm, I guess. She looked tired, and I know what it's like to miss your bus and simply want to get home." I lifted one shoulder. "I was glad to help."

He studied me for a moment, then nodded. He sat down a few feet away and pulled out his phone. Feeling strangely disappointed, I went back to digging for my earbuds, thinking I would have to clean out my purse on the weekend. I couldn't find a thing in it.

"Maybe you need a smaller purse."

I paused my digging, knowing I had been talking out loud again. Living alone, I did that a lot, although I tried to refrain from doing so out in public.

I glanced over at the man, startled at his close proximity.

Had he moved?

"I'll take that under advisement," I replied dismissively, then bent my head.

"I'd like to take you to dinner."

I almost dropped my purse but managed to grab it before it fell from my lap.

"I beg your pardon?"

He chuckled. "You're exceptionally polite. I like that. I said I would like to take you to dinner."

"Um, thank you, but no."

My response didn't seem to faze him. He lifted one shoulder casually.

"All right."

He leaned back, crossing his leg over his knee, and draped his arm along the back of the bench. He was near enough I could feel his warmth and smell his expensive cologne. Ocean breezes and citrus filled my nose. I liked it.

"Is it because you don't know me?"

His words jolted me back to reality. "I'm sorry?"

"Why you won't have dinner with me—because you don't know me."

"Yes, that's part of it. It's not advisable to walk off with strangers you meet at a bus stop."

He nodded. "Good point."

"You could be a stalker or a serial killer for all I know."

"I could be. Or a mobster. They're pretty scary. Trigger happy too from what I've seen."

"Had lots of dealings with mobsters, have you?" I asked sarcastically.

He stared at me. "I watch TV," he replied haughtily. "I'm aware of how they operate."

My lips twitched, but I stayed silent.

I moved my hand around, locating my earbuds. "Finally," I muttered. I slipped them on, plugging them into my phone. I began scrolling through my playlists when one earbud was pulled from my ear.

"Hey!" I gasped.

"I'm not," he said firmly.

"Not what?" I snatched my bud from his fingers—his long, incredibly sexy fingers.

"A stalker or a serial killer. Even a mobster."

"I see."

"I'm a nice guy."

"You're annoying."

"Only because you insist on ignoring me. You make me notice you, then you blow me off."

I felt the flare of anger. "Listen, buddy. I didn't try to get your attention. I didn't even notice you. I was helping someone—that's all."

He laid a hand over his heart in mock indignation. "You didn't notice me? I saw you the instant you came around the corner. When you whistled, I took it as a sign."

"Well, take this as a sign. Have a nice night." I turned my back to him and slid my buds into my ears. I hit play blindly, letting the music drown out all the other noise—including him. He was an arrogant ass—good-looking, but insufferable.

A moment later, his phone appeared in front of me. On the screen was a kitten, its paws together as if begging. *Forgive me*, the caption read.

Damn it. *A kitten?* This guy was good.

I turned around, noticing he was even closer—right beside me. I yanked out my buds. "Ever heard of personal space?"

"Yes. But you smell good. Really good."

I resisted the urge to tell him he did too. Instead, I shook my head in exasperation. "Persistent as well, I see."

"Is that worse than being a serial killer?"

"Right now, yes."

"I think I've figured out how to get you to have dinner with me."

"Is that right? Fast thinker."

He nodded, tapping his forehead. "It's a three-step plan."

"I see."

He held up a finger. "One, to get you to talk to me again. I've accomplished that. Two, introduce myself so we're no longer strangers. Then we move on to number three and head to dinner."

I shook my head, trying not to laugh. He was impossible—and

getting more impossible to resist. Every time he smiled, his dimples popped. His eyes crinkled. His expression turned mischievous. He was very sexy.

He held out his hand. "I'm Mitchell. Mitchell Emerson."

With a slight sigh of resignation, I slid my hand into his. His long fingers curled around my palm, strong yet gentle.

"Amanda Clifford."

"Lovely to meet you, Amanda. Do your friends call you Mandy?"

"Yes."

"Great. Now, Mandy, how about dinner?"

"Are you always this persistent?"

"When I want something, yes."

"Look, Mitchell—"

He interrupted me. "Mitch. My friends call me Mitch."

I sighed and tried again. "Look, *Mitchell*, I appreciate the offer, but the bottom line is you're still a stranger. I don't know you, or anything about you. I can't simply go to dinner with you because you asked."

He tilted his head and studied me. Once again, the light caught his coppery curls, and I had to stop myself from reaching out and seeing if they were as soft as they looked. I had a feeling he'd like that and use it to his advantage.

"That's the point of a date, I think," he stated. "To get to know each other."

"Now it's a date?"

"It is? Awesome!"

I started to laugh. "Stop twisting my words around. I don't know you. I am not going out to dinner with you."

"It's time to move on to number three of my plan. The big guns."

"Which is?"

He held out his phone. "References."

I stared at the screen.

My son Mitchell is a gentleman. He will behave or face my wrath. Enjoy your dinner!

I gaped at him. "Your mother?"
He tapped the screen. "There's more."
I glanced down.

My big brother is a pain, but the sweetest guy you'll ever meet. Text me if you want more deets. 555-123-4567 - Kris

I began to laugh. He tapped the screen again.

Mitch Emerson is an upstanding citizen and one hell of a golfer. That's really all I can say about him without incriminating myself. Oh, he has great taste in wine. - Sincerely, Joseph Talbot

I looked up, one eyebrow raised.

"My best friend," he explained. "I can give you all their cell phone numbers or I have my boss on speed dial. He'd vouch for me."

"Why?" I asked. "Why are you going to all this trouble?"

His expression turned serious. "I saw you come around the corner and all I could think about was getting to meet you."

I shook my head in confusion. "Again, why?"

"You want honest?"

"Yes, I like honest."

"I thought you were the prettiest woman I had ever seen. Then I saw you help that lady, which meant you were also kind. I found your whistle extremely sexy. And I love your legs. They really do it for me. Roll all that together, and I liked the package." He sucked in a deep breath and paused. "So, Amanda, I was hoping maybe you liked my package and would have dinner with me."

I burst out laughing at his words. He had the grace to look ashamed, even if his eyes were dancing with mirth.

"Do you, Amanda? Do you like the looks of my package?"

I couldn't resist. I didn't want to. Persistent, annoying, and sexy as hell. Plus, he thought *I* was sexy and he liked my legs. Two firsts for me.

"It's at least worth checking out."

He leaned forward, grinning. "I guarantee you'll be satisfied."

"Is that so?"

"Is that a yes?"

I gave in. I was hungry, and dinner with a companion sounded nice. "Yes."

"Can you recommend a good restaurant?" he asked. "I only moved here a few days ago, and I don't know many places."

I thought about it for a moment. "There's an Italian place just down the street."

"I love pasta."

"Me too." I did, and the restaurant was within walking distance. If things went south, I was still close to the bus stop and it was in an area I was familiar with.

He stood and held out his hand. "You just made my night, Mandy."

I allowed him to pull me from the bench.

I had a feeling he might have just made mine too.

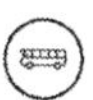

The streets were busy, people rushing to get to dinner, the theater, or one of the various other events happening in the city on a Friday night. Mitch stayed close, his hand hovering over the small of my back, as we headed toward the restaurant. When I was jostled a couple of times, he cursed low in his throat. Sliding his arm around my waist, he drew me into his side. I gazed up at him, arching one eyebrow.

"To keep you safe," he said to my unspoken question.

I didn't argue or move away. Tucked beside him felt...*right*. His six-foot-plus frame towered over me. I was average height for a woman, but I felt small and safe beside him. His warmth sank into my skin, and every time he pulled me closer as a group passed us, I could smell his incredible scent. I was almost disappointed when we reached the restaurant and he released me.

Luckily, it was thinning out as people hurried to the next phase of their evening, and we were seated right away. I slid into the booth, trying not to grin as he stood, his gaze bouncing between the two sides of the table.

"I want to sit beside you."

I slid closer to the wall. "Be my guest."

"But I like to watch the expressions on your face when you talk. They captivate me."

His words caught me off guard. I wasn't used to the easy compliments he threw out. Yet, they seemed completely sincere.

He slid in opposite me. "Dinner here, dessert there."

"What if we don't make it to dessert?" I teased.

"Then I'll move to the bar and drown my sorrows."

"Isn't that a little overboard? We just met."

He reached across the table and clasped my hand. Turning it over, he traced the veins on the thin skin of my wrist gently. His touch made me shiver. He met my inquisitive gaze. "I think our meeting is going to prove to be a significant moment in my life."

My breath caught in my throat. Our eyes met and held. Sincerity blazed from the depths of ocean blue staring into my startled gaze.

I opened my mouth, but no words came out. I had no idea how to respond to such a profound statement.

Mitch bent low and lifted my hand to his mouth. He pressed a soft, lingering kiss to the skin.

"Sorry, I get carried away. My mom and sister tell me to slow my roll all the time."

I felt a flash of trepidation. "You pick up a lot of women?"

He shook his head firmly. "No. I swear to God I am not a player. I just make decisions fast. Moving here, changing jobs, picking an apartment. Going after the prettiest woman who could stop a train with her whistle and sexy legs. That sort of thing." He winked. "Especially, the pretty woman."

I felt myself grow warm under his gaze.

He chuckled. "I really love your expressive face." He sat back, but didn't release my hand. "Surely, your previous boyfriends told you how incredibly pretty you are."

I slid back my hand, ignoring the way his fingers flexed, trying to hold it to his.

"Not really."

"Then they must have been blind. And totally stupid."

I shook my head, surprised by his words once more. "You can't say things like that. You don't even know me."

He smirked, draping his arm over the back of the booth. "The evening is young, Mandy. I plan to rectify that."

"One night isn't going to change anything."

He shook his head, signaling for the waiter. "That, sweetheart, is where you're wrong. One night is going to change everything."

Mitch

The subdued light in the restaurant played off Mandy's face, highlighting the curve of her cheeks. I wasn't joking when I told her I had noticed her, the instant she came around the corner. Her bright red coat had caught my eye, and her long, shapely legs made me sit up straighter and take notice. Her dark brown hair swung freely around her shoulders, and she walked with a sexy, easy grace. When she put her fingers to her mouth and whistled, I was a goner. I was on my feet and headed toward her without another thought. Watching her fist bump the air when the woman caught her bus, made me grin. I was certain she didn't even realize she had made the gesture. When she sat down and rubbed her calves, it was all I could do not to drop to my knees in front of her and offer to do it for her.

When I approached her and she lifted her face to mine, my breath caught. Big, mossy green eyes, creamy skin, and lips that were meant to be kissed—by me—greeted me. Her smile was killer, full and wide, even when she was telling me off. Her protests and vain attempts to ignore me only spurred me on. I wanted—needed—to spend some time with her. There was something about her that drew me in. I wanted to figure out what that something was, and once I had made up my mind, I never missed a goal.

And Amanda Clifford was now a huge goal.

On our walk to the restaurant, the feel of her nestled into my side was better than I had hoped. She fit there perfectly. She wasn't a skinny woman that felt like a skeleton. She was curvy and sexy, and I liked how she molded to my body. If I turned my head to look at her, I caught a whiff of her shampoo—fruity and sweet. Or maybe it was her. I was good with either one. I wanted more of it.

After confirming she liked wine, I ordered a good bottle of red, and we studied the menu. I kept looking up, catching her staring back at me. Her gaze would drop, prompting me to grin. She felt it too. The intense chemistry that hit me the instant our eyes met. I wanted to explore it.

I wanted to explore her. Every single delectable inch of her.

"Anything look good to you?" she asked.

"Yes."

She glanced up, her eyebrows lifted in question.

"Oh sorry, you meant the menu?"

She furrowed her brow. "What did you think I meant?"

I leaned closer over the table, smiling. "You. You look good to me."

Her cheeks flooded, diffusing her skin with a flush of color that only heightened my attraction to her. She lifted the menu higher, hiding her face. I plucked the offending folder from her hands, setting it aside.

"I don't like it when you hide. You are far too pretty for me not to look at."

"I haven't decided yet," she objected.

"I have. We're having the chef's special menu."

"Oh, are we? What if I don't like it?"

"Then I'll order you something else. Tonight is all about spontaneity, so we'll let him decide what we eat. Any allergies I should inform them about? Strong dislikes?"

She pursed her lips, then shrugged. "No."

"Okay, then. I hope dinner is amazing." I lifted my glass in a toast. "Just like meeting you."

She lifted her glass, touching it to mine. "You're very direct."

"I am."

"You say things—things I'm not sure how to take."

I relaxed back against the leather banquette and studied her in the dim light. There was something so intriguing about her. I wanted to know her—all about her. And for the first time in a long while, I wanted a woman to know me.

"You'll get used to it. I speak my mind, especially when I'm pleased."

She hesitated, then spoke. "And I please you?"

"Oh, sweetheart. You have no idea."

She shook her head, but the smile on her lips said it all.

CHAPTER TWO

MANDY

He was confident, direct, and blunt. High-handed and bossy. He was also the most courteous date I'd ever had. He made certain I liked everything the waiter brought us, ensured my water and wine glasses were always topped up, listened carefully when I spoke, and he asked so many questions, it was obvious he was listening to every word I said. We talked about a variety of subjects, but never touched on anything too personal. He was well read and intelligent, and we discovered a mutual like of museums and weekend flea markets. We also had the common bond of loving historical architecture. He told me he was a consultant and had started a new long-term project that week. I worried the inside of my cheek when he told me that information. He smiled knowingly.

"I'm here for at least a year, Mandy. Maybe more. I'm not a hit and run kind of guy."

"All right," I replied, slightly mollified. A year suddenly felt like a short span of time.

"What do you do?"

"I'm a PA in a busy architectural firm for now."

His eyebrows rose slightly. "Architectural firm?"

"Yes. Parson Planners."

He took a sip of his drink and frowned. "I see."

"I'm looking for another job, though."

"Why?" he asked, narrowing his eyes. "You don't like your current job? Are the people you work for unkind?"

"My direct boss isn't exactly my number one fan. We don't get along. She can be, ah, difficult."

"Have you ever told her off?"

I laughed, because I'd done so in my head many times. "No, I need my paycheck. I do give in and sneak a piece of toffee when she berates me—which is daily."

He looked confused.

"We aren't allowed to keep snacks at our desk. I hide the toffee under my Post-it notes. I get sick enjoyment eating it knowing it would piss her off."

He threw back his head in laughter. "I think you need a new job."

"I've been looking, and I hope to find something soon." I sighed. "I might go back to school. Being a PA wasn't what I planned."

"I see. What was the plan?"

"I wanted to be a teacher. But my mom got sick and I left school to help her. When she passed, I was lost for a while. I couldn't find my path or make any decisions. This job came up five months ago, and I took it."

He covered my hand, squeezing it gently. "I'm sorry for your loss, Mandy."

I blinked away the sudden moisture in my eyes and cleared my throat.

"She was a dancer. I always loved to watch her performances."

"Explains the great legs."

I chuckled. "I got her legs, but not her coordination. She moved like the air. She used to tease me that I was born with two left feet."

He met my eyes, his gaze intense. "I like how you move."

I had no idea how to reply to his statement.

I looked down at the table. "I still miss her."

"I'm sure you do." He was quiet, and I could feel it as he studied me. "But you're ready to move on from your job?"

I met his gaze. "I think so. I'm never going anywhere there, and I think I'm ready to move forward."

A smile played on his lips. "I arrived just in time, then."

I tried to hide my own smile.

I failed.

He stood and excused himself. I watched him walk away, unable to help noticing that his ass was spectacular. High, round, and firm. I wanted to grab it and see what it felt like under my hands. I was certain it would be perfection.

When he returned, he smiled widely as he slid back into the booth. "That's taken care of."

I frowned. "Problem?"

He shook his head and smirked. "Not anymore."

"I don't understand."

He grinned. "Nothing to worry about. Something regarding work I had to take care of. Now, I can concentrate on the task at hand."

"Eating dinner?"

He cocked one eyebrow at me. "Getting to know you and making sure you want to see me again."

I had to laugh as I picked up my glass. His friend was correct—he had great taste in wine. It was smooth and full-bodied. Sort of like Mitch.

He never stopped. His questions were endless, his humor contagious. He was droll and amusing, disparaging about himself without being too serious. He told me funny stories of his friend Joseph who he had known his whole life, his sister Kris, and his mom and dad. He kept me in stitches with his wicked imitations of when they would get into trouble and his mother would start to yell.

At one point, I left the table to go to the ladies room. As I washed my hands, I studied myself in the mirror, unsure what it was that he found so attractive. Brown hair, green eyes, and a figure much too curvy to be called slim was all I saw. However, he seemed to disagree.

Every time I glanced up, he was staring at me, his frank appraisal making me warm. His eyes followed my movements, watching my fork transfer food to my mouth. He studied my hands when I used them to emphasize a point. More than once, he reached out to touch my hand or arm, even leaning over the table to push a stray curl behind my ear.

Not one prone to physical contact, I was shocked to discover I liked his affectionate gestures.

When I arrived back at our table, he stood in one of his old-fashioned gestures, waiting until I slid into the booth. I shivered a little at the contrast in temperatures. The restaurant seemed chilly compared to the restroom. He frowned, and before I could object, slipped his suit jacket off and leaned over me to drape it around my shoulders. He slid in next to me, sitting so close, our thighs pushed together. Casually, he leaned his arm on the back of the booth, his warmth soaking into my side. His jacket was smooth, and his scent surrounded and enveloped me.

I liked it.

The waiter brought our dessert and coffee, not at all surprised to find us on the same side of the booth.

Mitch slid his fork into the dense cheesecake, lifting it to his mouth. His sexy, full mouth that had teased me all night. His eyes shut as he chewed and swallowed. He cut off another slice, holding out his fork.

"You have to try this. It is amazing."

He had done that the whole night. Spearing small bites off his plate, offering them to me, watching my mouth intently as I tasted and swallowed. He licked his lips often, and more than once, shifted in his seat. It was oddly sensual for him to feed me.

I opened my mouth to accept the bite, then shut my eyes and let the creamy, sweet taste coat my tongue. The tart blackberries heightened the flavor, and a small groan escaped my lips.

Opening my eyes, I met his staggered gaze. His fork was frozen, hovering over his plate.

"Mitch?" I asked. "What is it?"

His fork fell to his plate with a clatter. He turned fully, facing me.

"What *is* it?" he repeated. "You really have to ask that?"

I shook my head, confused. "Yes?"

He pressed nearer, and without a thought, I turned into him. We were so close I could feel his hot breath on my face. Feel the warmth of his body pressed to mine.

"It's you," he growled softly. "Your enticing mouth and erotic sounds. The way you look at me. Your captivating eyes." He stroked his knuckles down my face. "Your expressions and your laughter." His voice dropped further. "I want to kiss you right now. Please tell me I can."

My breath faltered. I didn't know this man. I had met him a few short hours ago. But somewhere between his directness, his teasing, our non-stop conversation, and his sexy, over-the-top commentary, that had ceased to matter. I wanted him.

And I wanted him to kiss me.

Senseless.

He smirked—wide, knowing, and confident.

"Not a problem, sweetheart."

Then his mouth was on mine.

I didn't think we could get closer. I was wrong. He yanked me to him as if I was a lifesaver and he was a drowning man. His lips slanted over mine, demanding, yet tender. Our mouths moved, sliding and molding to each other. His tongue slid along my bottom lip, and with a sigh, I opened for him.

Desire, hot and intense, exploded. His taste overwhelmed me. He fisted my hair, tilting my head, going deeper. He consumed me. His tongue stroked and teased. Tasted and explored. He tugged me with both hands, almost pulling me onto his lap, his hand on my hip, curving to form to my body. He surrounded me, and everything outside the booth ceased to exist. There was nothing, nobody, but him and me. His chest rumbled in pleasure as I weaved my fingers into the short hairs at the nape of his neck, playing with the strands, and caressing his skin.

With a low moan, he pulled away, dragging his lips along my cheek to my ear. "You are even more than I hoped," he murmured. He teased the skin of my neck, making me shudder in delight.

"Your skin is so soft," he breathed into my ear. "I want to know how it feels against mine. All of it."

"Mitch," I whispered. "We just met."

"I know," he acknowledged, his mouth ghosting over my cheek, kissing me again. "Tell me you feel this connection."

"Yes."

"Come to my hotel."

My breathing hitched. "I... We..."

He shook his head. "I expect nothing. I promise. I just want you alone. I want to kiss you properly."

I lifted one eyebrow in disbelief and ran my fingers over my lips, still feeling his mouth. "That wasn't properly?"

He captured my hand in his and kissed the knuckles. "More, then. I want to kiss you more."

I hesitated.

He smiled and once again stroked my cheek. "It's fine, Mandy. I understand. I wouldn't normally move so fast, but I have to admit, I have never wanted a woman as much as I want you." He removed his arm, and slid back, picking up his fork. "I can be patient. You'll be worth the wait." He smiled. "We'll be worth the wait."

His words disarmed me. I was shocked how much I immediately missed his warmth. A flicker of disappointment went through me at his easy acceptance of my hesitation.

Even though, I knew that was silly, I should've been grateful he didn't push the issue.

Right?

We finished sharing dessert, and when the bill came, I picked up my purse.

"Don't even think about it," he informed me with a glare. "I asked you to dinner. When we're on a date, or wherever, I will take care of the bill."

"Is this a date?" I asked.

"Yes. Our first of many." He stood, extending his hand. "Will you walk with me for a bit before I put you in a cab to go home?"

"I can take the bus."

He rolled his eyes, tugging me from the booth. "You obviously haven't been treated very well by your old boyfriends. The likelihood of me allowing you to take a bus home after a date is about the same as me being able to resist kissing you again tonight."

"So, not good then?"

He grinned and dropped a hard, fast kiss to my mouth.

"Impossible."

We left the restaurant hand in hand. There was no false pretense about him as he tucked me close to his side. The streets had thinned out, but as usual, there were still lots of people milling around.

"Where to?"

He smiled. "At the risk of you walking away, the bar in my hotel is on the top floor. Great view at night and it's only a couple of blocks away. We could have a drink, and I promise to escort you downstairs after and send you home in a taxi."

The evening had gotten cooler, the bite of winter approaching in the air. Sitting in a bar talking to Mitch sounded a lot better than walking in the night breeze.

"Okay."

He steered us across the street, toward his hotel. He asked about restaurants around the area, other amenities, and where I lived.

"Have you found a place yet?" I asked, after answering his questions. "Do you rent or lease?"

"Since I'm self-employed and often my work-contract is brief, I usually stay in hotels. But here, I wanted a short-term lease. I looked at a few today and found one I liked."

"Where is your office?"

He waved the air. "Downtown."

I chuckled. "Maybe our companies are rivals."

He laughed. "Maybe. We won't discuss work. Make that part easier." He pulled me closer and pressed a kiss to my head. "I'd much rather talk about you, Mandy. I find you fascinating."

I laughed lightly. "Then you need to get out more."

He chuckled and stopped at the entrance to a swanky hotel. He turned to face me. "Still okay for that drink?"

I stared up at him. His eyes were incredible. Icy blue, intense, and piercing. The color belied the warmth they held as he regarded me, though. There was nothing glacial about his gaze. It was pure heat. I felt his desire he held in check. The way his body responded to me. The way I was responding to him.

"I haven't been with anyone in a long time, Mitch. Since before my mother died."

His grip tightened. "I told you already that I'm not a player, Mandy. This isn't the norm for me. But then again, I don't think you're the norm."

"I'm not?"

"No." He shook his head, pulling me closer. "I think you're going to be the exception." His eyes dropped to my mouth. "God knows I want to be that for you."

The breath left my lungs in a long shudder.

"Maybe we could have that drink in your room?"

A slow smile spread across his face. "Yeah, sweetheart. We could do that."

We barely made it into his room when he was on me. His mouth was hungry, his kisses deep, passionate, and consuming. His tongue was wicked and relentless—exploring me, curling and sliding with mine, feasting on my taste. His hands never ceased their exploration. He touched me everywhere, outlining my curves, feathering over my skin, gripping my ass. He pulled me to him tight, our chests melded, our bodies aligned.

I could feel him. Everywhere. His desire. His need. His want.

For me.

It was overwhelming.

My own desire burned hot. Hotter than it ever had for any man. His muscles bunched under my touch. His copper hair was soft as the ends curled around my fingers. His cock trapped between us was large and stiff. He trembled as I ran my hand over the bulge.

"I promised you a drink," he rasped, dragging his lips across my cheek.

"I'm not thirsty."

"I fucking am," he responded. "For you. Your taste. Give me back your mouth, Mandy."

The room spun. All of my senses tunneled down to him. Us. His body. Heat built within me. A slow, intense burn that melted me from the inside out. I was achy, filled with need. It felt as if my nerves were on the outside of my body and Mitch knew where each trigger lay. He stroked them, fanning the flames until I was ready to burst.

With a low growl, I pushed his jacket from his shoulders and fumbled with the buttons of his shirt. I yanked on his sleeves, smiling at the sound of the material rendering. I tugged at his belt, suddenly desperate to feel him.

"Easy, tiger." He nipped at my lips, a dark chuckle sounding in the room. "You've got me, baby. Leave me some clothes intact."

"I want you naked."

"Jesus, you're wild, sweetheart." His hand covered mine as he helped guide my fingers.

I opened his belt and slid his pants down his legs within seconds. Then I dropped to my knees.

Mitch

I stared down in shock. A few hours ago, I had planned on a few drinks in the bar, maybe room service, and a quiet night alone. Never had I imagined meeting Mandy or having her on her knees in front of me.

Her hands slid up the back of my thighs, tugging down my boxers. My aching cock sprang free, slapping against my stomach. Mandy gazed up at me, her eyes huge in the dim light.

"Sweetheart, you don't—"

I groaned as she wrapped her hand around me, shaking her head.

"I want to."

Then her mouth was on me.

My head fell back against the wall with a dull thud. Warm, wet, and teasing. Whistling was only one of her wicked mouth's talents. Her tongue ran along my shaft, swirling around the heavy head, making me hiss in pleasure. I wove my hand into her hair and cupped the back of her head, my fingers moving restlessly on her scalp. She gripped my ass, pressing on my skin to draw me deeper into her mouth.

"Fuck," I groaned. "Mandy, sweetheart, you can't... I can't..."

Pleasure racked my body. My legs began to shake. When she sucked my balls into her mouth, rolling them around, teasing them with her tongue, before cupping them and sliding my cock back into her warmth, I shouted her name.

I pushed on her shoulders, forcing her back. I bent low and lifted her under her arms, and tossed her on the bed.

She smiled at me mischievously. "You didn't like that?"

"I fucking loved your mouth on me. But I want to be inside you."

She ran a finger over her lips. "Next time, then."

I groaned at her actions. She was sexy.

"You have way too many clothes on."

She stretched her arms out. "You want to do something about that?"

In seconds, I had her clothes peeled off, leaving her in wisps of racy red lace.

"Jesus, Mandy. You're stunning."

She smiled and drew up her legs, tugging the lace down her shapely calves. I fit my hands around her knees, caressing the silky-smooth skin. With a flick of her wrist, her breasts were bare, the nipples hard. Teasingly, I ran my fingers over them, watching her shiver in anticipation.

"Are you sure, sweetheart?"

"Yes."

I tugged on her knees, and gently pushed open her legs. "Then show me."

Her pussy was wet, glistening, and beckoning me.

I didn't refuse the invitation.

I eased between her thighs, hovering over her naked, inviting body. Lowering my face to hers, I kissed her deeply. Our chests touched, her soft, warm breasts pressing into the hard angles of my body.

I explored her inch by inch, taking my time, ignoring the fiery need to claim her—to bury myself inside her and possess her wholly. It was like nothing I had ever experienced. Not simply a physical need, but an emotional one as well. I wanted every single part of her.

Her neck was so delicate under my tongue. Her nipples small points of pleasure that made her gasp when I drew them into my mouth. Every inch of her was delectable, and I wanted to feast on her for hours. Sliding my fingers through her wetness, she cried out my name, coming fast when I sucked at her swollen clit, flicking it with my tongue.

I rose on my heels to stare down at her. Her dark hair spilled across her pillow like a wave. Her cheeks were flushed, her chest heaving as she reached for me.

"Condom," I groaned. "I need a condom."

"Where?" She gasped.

"Drawer. Beside you."

Blindly, she reached into the drawer, finding one and handing it to me with a grin. I ignored the flash of jealousy that this scenario had occurred before. That she had handed another man a condom with that smile on her face. The past was the past. From now on, it would only be me inside her. I was determined it be that way.

I rolled on the latex, bracing myself above her.

"Remember what I said earlier, sweetheart? One night is going to change everything." I nudged at her entrance, trying not to moan at the heat that teased me. "Once I'm inside you, it's done. You're mine. You understand that?"

She wrapped her legs around my waist. "And you're mine."

I slid inside, the intense pleasure making me growl. Our gazes locked, a silent understanding passing between us. We both felt it. Neither of us was going to fight it.

"Yes, I'm yours."

I tucked Mandy into my side, sighing in contentment. I had made love to her twice. Each time was incredible. It was as if our bodies had been waiting for each other. We moved together as though we had done it a thousand times, yet the newness and excitement of it was there. Our passion was raw and vivid. The desire was rampant.

I ran my fingers down her arm and pressed a kiss to her head. She mumbled something I didn't catch. I slipped a finger under her chin and lifted her face. Her lips were swollen and red. There were scratches on her neck from my stubble. A small, purple mark was at the base of her neck from where I had marked her. She was truly beautiful.

"What was that, sweetheart?"

"I asked if you wanted me to stay."

I tightened my embrace. "Fucking right I do."

She chuckled, burrowing closer. Never much of a cuddler, I was surprised how much I liked having her close. "Okay, just checking."

"You don't want to leave, do you?"

She lifted her head again. "No! I just didn't want you to feel...obligated."

I laughed, kissing the end of her nose affectionately. "Obligated is not what I'm feeling right now. Trust me when I say that."

"I do trust you."

I felt a small fission of guilt that I tamped down quickly. I would deal with that soon enough. For now, I simply wanted to bask in the moment. In her. In us.

"What are you doing tomorrow?" I asked.

She peeked over my shoulder. "You mean later today?"

I glanced at the clock. "Holy shit; it's three o'clock. I've kept you awake a long time."

She nuzzled into my neck. "We were busy." Her hand slipped down my chest, ghosted lower, and wrapped around my cock. I was already hard for her again. "I don't think we're finished either."

"I don't think I have any more condoms."

She heaved a long sigh. "Don't you have a spare in your wallet? What kind of wild bachelor are you? I could report you and get you taken out of the club, you know."

I chuckled at her wit. "First off, I told you I am not a player. I carry a couple in case, but we just used them." I nudged her nose playfully. "Usually, one is enough. Two is rare. Needing a third? I don't think that has ever happened to me."

"Me, either."

She continued to stroke me, making me groan in need. "I could call down to the front desk and get some sent up?"

She grimaced. "That would be embarrassing. We can do other stuff," she whispered. "Lots of other stuff."

I arched my eyebrow at her. "Oh, really? What sort of other *stuff* are we talking about, Ms. Clifford?"

She pushed on my chest, straddling me. She gazed down with an impish grin.

"Why don't I show you, Mr. Emerson?"

I gripped her hips. "Excellent idea. I love show and tell."

CHAPTER THREE

MANDY

I rolled over, blinking in the morning light. A hard body followed my movements; strong arms pulled me back into a warm embrace. Lips traced a line of gentle kisses on my neck, making me smile sleepily.

Mitch.

Flashes of last night danced through my head. Meeting him. Dinner. Going to his hotel. Having sex.

Lots of sex.

Lots of amazing, mind-blowing sex.

At one point while I dozed, he'd run to the all-night drugstore across the street, returning with more condoms. They'd been well used. The dull ache in my body proved that.

"Morning, sweetheart," he breathed into my ear, tugging me to him. "Sleep well?"

Well didn't describe it. I had slept like the dead, my usual tossing and turning non-existent. Still, I couldn't resist teasing him.

"Well, I would have, if it wasn't for that god-awful snoring. You should get medical attention for that."

In a second, I was on my back, him hovering over me. He glared, and his blue eyes narrowed in the morning light as his hair fell over his forehead.

"I don't snore."

"Hmmph."

He smoothed his hands over my arms, lifted them over my head, and locked them into place. "Take that back, Amanda Clifford."

"Or?"

"You'll be sorry." His voice was low and threatening, but the amused glint in his eyes assured me I was in no danger. His cock, massive and hard, let me know exactly how he planned to punish me for my teasing.

I was fine with that.

I arched my back, spreading my legs. He settled between them with a satisfied smirk. "Ready to take your punishment for your insolence, sweetheart?"

I bit my lip and wrapped my legs around his hips. "Yes, sir."

He groaned, lowering his head. "You are going to be the death of me, woman." His mouth touched mine. "But what a way to go."

I sipped the coffee Mitch ordered with breakfast, enjoying the dark brew. Nibbling on a piece of toast, I watched in rapt fascination as he devoured a stack of pancakes. He had already demolished a plate of bacon and eggs, and I saw him eyeing up my scrambled eggs with interest.

He grinned, as I pulled my plate closer.

"Don't worry, sweetheart. I know you need some sustenance. We'll get something else to fill me up in a while."

"Oh?"

He wiped his mouth, and drained his coffee, then refilled his cup. "You said you had no plans for today?"

"Nothing big. Errands, laundry."

He laced our fingers together. "Spend the day with me. I'm going to the new place to make sure my boxes arrived, then I need to get a couple of things. You know the city better than I do. We can do your errands at the same time, and laundry can happen tomorrow, maybe?" he asked, sounding hopeful.

"Your boxes?"

"I have some things that go everywhere with me. Not a lot, but some pictures, clothes, etc. They arrived the day after I did and were being held until I found a place."

"How did you get it so quickly?"

He grinned. "Not my first time at the rodeo. I saw what I liked, signed, paid my deposit with the condition of immediate possession. It was empty, so it wasn't an issue."

"Decisive."

He lifted my hand to his mouth. "When I want something, yes. Please, Mandy. I want to be with you today. I'm not ready to let you go yet."

I glanced down. I was wearing his shirt from last night. My clothes were in a pile on the floor, no doubt wrinkled and unwearable.

He chuckled, knowing what I was thinking. "We can go to your place and you can change if you want. Then to my new place, have lunch, just spend some more time together. Please."

I couldn't resist his pleading gaze. His blue eyes danced in the sunlight, his hair all over the place from where I'd had my hands buried in it. His scruff was thicker this morning, the coppery hairs bright in the light. His smile was warm and kind, his voice rich and inviting.

"Okay."

His smile widened. "Great."

I shifted, trying not to grimace. Mitch noticed immediately, setting down his coffee.

"Are you sore? Did I hurt you?" he asked, his tone laced with concern.

I tilted my head, studying him. Despite his passion, his strength, or his desire, he had been nothing but gentle with me. Even when he lost himself with lust, I had felt the reverence in his caresses.

"No," I assured him. "It's, ah, just been a while, and we went at it, ah, pretty often."

He grinned, his dimples popping. "That's an understatement. A record for me, if I'm being honest." He shook his head. "I'm insatiable when it comes to you."

I felt my cheeks flush.

He leaned over the table, running his fingers over my face. "I don't want you sore. How about soak in the tub and some Tylenol while I firm up the times with some delivery people?"

"No need to fuss. A hot shower will be fine."

His eyes flashed. "Maybe I could wash your back?"

"Maybe."

He handed me my plate with a wink. "Eat up, sweetheart. You're going to need it."

I walked around Mitch's large apartment eyeing the rooms with admiration. I liked my place, but my entire apartment could fit into the bedroom here alone. I stood at the window, admiring the view, listening to the sound of Mitch's voice as he spoke with the delivery people.

It was an amazing apartment. Spacious, clean, with a great view, and a kitchen that made me want to start cooking as soon as I saw it.

Mitch had stepped behind me and wrapped his arm around my waist, pulling me close.

"You like to cook, sweetheart?"

"Yeah, I do."

"Me, too," he stated. "I find it relaxing, but it's not fun to cook for one all the time."

"No," I agreed. "It's not."

"We can cook together. Here."

I tilted up my head, meeting his eyes. "Sure glad you're slowing your roll."

He chuckled and kissed me hard. "When it comes to you, that simply isn't possible."

I sighed as I looked out the window. If anyone had told me yesterday I'd be there with Mitch, after spending the night with him, I would have laughed at them. Yet, there I was.

I rubbed my temples, still feeling disbelief. Mitch seemed too good to be true. Warm, open, caring, sexy. Frank and forward. Honest about what he wanted.

And it seemed he wanted me. But for how long?

His arms wound around me. "What are you looking so pensive for?" he murmured. "What's wrong?"

"Nothing. I was just thinking about things."

"*Nothing*," he scoffed. "Try again, sweetheart. You look worried."

I was silent, and he spun me in his arms, his face serious. "Talk to me."

"What am I doing here, Mitch? What are *we* doing?"

His expression softened. "You're here because I wanted to make sure you liked the place I picked. I plan, *I hope*, you're here with me a lot, so I wanted your input. As to what we're doing—I'm going to call it starting a relationship. An important one. I know it's fast, and I can see you're feeling a little overwhelmed, but we'll figure it out." His arms tightened. "As long as it's what you want. I know it's what I want."

I searched his eyes. In the bright light, they were clear, as blue as the sky, and reflected tenderness and understanding even if his expression was anxious.

"How can you be so sure?"

He smiled, tucking a strand of hair behind my ear. "I just do. You caught my eye with your whistle. You intrigued me with your wit and the way you brushed me off. You bowled me over with your smile once you let me in a little. I have never felt about someone the way I feel about you."

"The lust you mean?"

He shook his head. "Not just the sex. Don't get me wrong—it was hands down the best sex I've ever had, but it was more than simply sex. You felt it, didn't you? That connection? The feeling as if you'd found something you'd been looking for and hadn't ever realized was missing?"

I had felt it. I could still feel it. When Mitch was close, I felt safe and protected. Cared for. Complete. It was both heady and scary at the same time. I nodded hesitantly.

"But?" he pressed.

"It's only for a while."

He smiled and passed his fingers over my cheek. "We'll figure it all out, sweetheart. I'm freelance. I can go wherever I want, stay however long I decide to stay."

"That's what worries me. You can leave anytime you want."

He cocked his head. "My mom always told me one day I would find a reason to settle. I think, maybe I have found my reason. I think you're my reason."

I felt my eyes widen. "That's a pretty profound statement to make considering you haven't even known me twenty-four hours."

"You get better every minute. I'm surprised I'm still standing with how much you affect me."

The deliveryman called his name, and he pressed a kiss to my head. "We have lots of time, Mandy. I'm not going anywhere, and now I've met you, I don't plan to. As long as we're together, we'll find our way. Now let me go sign off on the delivery and we can go find the most important item for this place."

I nodded. "Right. You'll need a sofa."

He shook his head.

"A desk?"

He shook his head once more with a smirk. "I need those too, but first a bed. A huge bed, so comfortable, you'll want to be in it with me every night."

With a wink, he hurried away. I turned back to the window, but this time, I was smiling.

Mitch admitted he hated shopping and wanted to get it done swiftly. I took him to a high-end furniture store in the area, somehow knowing only the best would do for him. When we walked out an hour later, my head was reeling, but he was happy. He'd chosen pieces with the same decisiveness he had displayed with everything else since I'd met him. A large sofa and chair were first in a deep wine colored fabric. A couple of bar stools for the counter were next, and then we spent the rest of the time bed shopping. He made me laugh as he tossed me on various mattresses, following me quickly to "test" them. The salesman walked away chuckling, telling Mitch to let him know when he found the right one. Mitch waved his hand, his mouth too busy kissing me to respond. But his odd method worked, and there was one bed we both agreed was perfect.

"Done," he announced. "The rest I'll pick up when we're exploring some flea markets and antique places over the next while."

I lifted my eyebrows in question. "Oh, we will?"

He pulled me off the bed with another passionate kiss. "Yep."

I didn't challenge him. I didn't want to. I liked him too much.

After lunch, we stood outside the restaurant, his arm tight around my waist. "Do you really have to go?"

"Yes."

"Can I see you later?"

I thought of all the laundry and errands I had to take care of. "Maybe tomorrow?"

"Perfect. I'll take my things to the new place and you can meet me there. I'll go wait for the furniture now."

"I still don't know how you managed to arrange delivery of the furniture so fast."

"Money talks. He said they were in stock; I simply paid a premium to get them faster. I hate waiting. Patience isn't my strongest point."

I smirked. "I've noticed."

He tucked a stray piece of hair behind my ear. "Are you sure you can't stay with me?"

"Mitch, I can't."

He lifted his arm, hailing a taxi. "Thought I'd ask one more time, in case I caught you off guard."

Something in his voice made me pause. "I want to, but I have to take care of some things. So, I'll see you tomorrow."

His eyes lit up, his dimples deepened, and his smile was bright. "That gives me something to look forward to."

He opened the door of the taxi and I slid in the back seat. He spoke with the driver for a moment, then pushed his way into the back seat, his broad shoulders filling the doorway.

"I've paid the fare."

"You didn't have to do that."

He frowned. "You need to get used to being treated well, Mandy. Expect nothing less than the best from me. You deserve it."

He grasped the back of my neck, pulled my mouth to his, and kissed me deeply. His tongue stroked mine possessively, his fingers caressing my scalp. He drew back with a smile. "You deserve only the best."

I stared at him, unsure how to reply.

"Can I call you later?" he asked, looking uncharacteristically nervous.

"I'll call you if you don't." I winked.

"That's my girl." He shut the door and tapped the passenger window so the driver rolled it down. Mitch leaned in.

"You have precious cargo. Make sure she arrives safely."

The driver laughed and with a wave, pulled away from the curb. I looked over my shoulder, watching Mitch disappear from my view, and wondered why I felt so sad to leave him.

"Do you really have to go?" Mitch groaned, pulling me closer, pressing light kisses to my neck.

"I've been here all afternoon. I have to get ready for work tomorrow. So do you, I assume."

I had to fight back the impulse to say *screw it* and stay with him in his big bed where he'd lured me to not long after I arrived. Saturday night and Sunday morning had been filled with his constant texts, funny gifs, and sweet messages. When he'd thrown open the door and pulled me inside, he had kissed me as if it had been weeks, not hours, since he'd seen me last. I had to drag him out of his place to do some grocery shopping, and once we returned and ate, he enticed me to his room.

He muttered a curse and rolled over, flinging an arm over his face. "Let's forget about work and stay here."

I laughed and slid from the bed, reaching for my leggings. "Nice, Mr. Bigshot. Maybe you can play hooky, but I can't. That new architect arrives tomorrow and Michelle will be on a tear." I picked up my shirt and shook out the wrinkles before pulling it over my head. "Did they have a welcoming committee for you when you started at your new place?" I chuckled. "I have an image of us all lining up when Mr. Mackenzie walks in, and curtsying to him. I think he's old enough to appreciate it."

"Why would you say that?"

"I helped unpack his things. He's obviously well-traveled, so I guessed he was older. And Michelle was in such a tizzy, I assume he is very well-known."

Mitch sat up and I took a minute to appreciate the view. Broad shoulders, well-defined pecs, and a six-pack made up his form. The light blanket draped across his lap did nothing to hide his erection that grew as I stared at him. He lifted one eyebrow, crossing his arms casually behind his head, showing off his fine body. His voice was low and husky. "Careful, Mandy. I won't let you out of here if you keep staring like that."

The thought of another round of sex with Mitch made me whimper. We were amazing together. He made me feel things I had never felt. I wanted to try everything with him, and he was only too happy to oblige.

I shook my head to clear the lustful thoughts.

"It's after seven. I have to get home."

He slid from the bed, grabbed his jeans, and pulled them on. I ogled his ass while he was bent over, trying not to grin. It was a great ass, and the left cheek was imprinted with my mark. It suited him.

"I'll call you a taxi," he said grudgingly, throwing me a look that brooked no argument.

I wandered into the main room and picked up my purse that had fallen to the floor. A large framed print behind the sofa caught my eye, and I drew closer to inspect it. It was a building, high and soaring, set against the backdrop of a large city. Bold, dynamic, unique.

Familiar, somehow.

I tugged it from behind the sofa, studying it. My gaze fell to the bottom corner and the *MM* slashed out in black pen.

Mitch cleared his throat behind me.

I turned and stared at him. "You're a fan of Mr. Mackenzie?"

"Um, not exactly."

"Why do you have his work then?"

He shuffled his feet, hanging his head, before lifting his face to meet my confused gaze.

"Because it's my work, Mandy. I'm Mr. Mackenzie."

CHAPTER FOUR

MANDY

After Mitch had dropped his bombshell, I stepped back, shocked, clutching the back of the sofa.

"What?"

"My full name is Mackenzie Mitchell Emerson. In the business world, I go by Mackenzie Mitchell. To my family and friends, I'm Mitch Emerson." He shrugged. "I hate the name Mackenzie. My mother had to use it to please her father at the time."

"Michelle called you Mr. Mackenzie."

Again, he shrugged. "That's her error. She must have heard my name incorrectly."

I narrowed my eyes, anger making my heart beat faster. "But you didn't bother to correct me."

He ran a hand through his hair. "I should have. When you said the name of the firm you worked for, I was shocked. What were the chances the woman I'd fallen for at the bus stop worked at the place I had just signed on to consult for?"

"But you didn't."

"I didn't want to risk you walking away. I wanted you to get to know me."

My voice rose in disbelief. "By *lying* to me. That is what you wanted me to know about you?"

"I didn't lie."

His words hit me, echoing ones I had heard in the past. I crossed my arms as the familiar feeling of unease seeped into my chest. My body shook with repressed anger.

"By not telling me the complete truth, *you did.* Are you aware there is a strict non-fraternization clause at the office? By not telling me, you've put my job at risk."

Shaking his head, he stepped nearer. "No, I called my lawyer on Friday night and checked. It's not in my contract. I'm a consultant."

I dragged in some much-needed oxygen. "It's in mine. Very clearly. No dating of fellow employees, management, consultants, or business associates of Parson Planners." I shook my head in disbelief. "Do you realize if Michelle or anyone at the office found out, I would lose my job? You know how much I need this job."

He furrowed his brow. "I'll have him recheck. We'll figure it out, sweetheart."

I gaped at him.

Figure it out?

"Do you think we're going forward, Mitch? That I'd simply accept your lies and move on?" I tried to stop the quiver in my voice and failed. Disappointment and sadness flooded my system. "I thought you were different. You seemed so open and honest. So...*real.* How do you think I would have felt tomorrow when you showed up at the office?" I covered my mouth and swallowed. "That would have been horrible."

He reached for me, but I stepped back, shaking my head. "Don't."

He held out his hands beseechingly. "I am real. What I feel is real. I should have told you. I swear to God I intended to tell you earlier. But then we got carried away. I wasn't going to let you leave without telling you tonight. I wouldn't have done that to you, Mandy."

I stared at him, my emotions high, and not believing his words.

"You said you thought I hadn't been treated right in the past. You were correct. My boyfriend of two years didn't treat me very well. I was always second for him—often third or fourth. Everything and everyone else was always more important. He constantly made excuses, and somehow made me feel it was my fault—every time. He lied and cheated on me, and when I confronted him, he said it was easier just to keep me around for when he was bored. I wasted two years of my life trying to be enough for someone who never thought I was enough to be honest or put me first."

"I will put you first."

I picked up my purse and coat. "No. By lying and omission, you've shown me your job is already more important. You made me feel things for you without knowing who you were. You took the choice from me. I can't do that again."

"Sweetheart, don't—"

I didn't let him finish. I held up my hand, trying hard not to break down in front of him. I indicated the space between us. "This never happened, Mitch or Mackenzie—whatever your name is. Tomorrow, you are going to pretend you never met me and you are not going to jeopardize my job. As much as I don't like it, I need it until I've saved enough to go back to school."

"I don't know if I can pretend not to know you."

I tossed my hair, pausing with my hand on the doorknob. "I can, because obviously, I never did. I have no idea who you really are, and frankly, I have no desire to do so any longer."

I walked out, ignoring his devastated expression and the way he hunched over the back of the sofa as if in physical pain.

And he let me go.

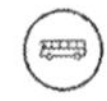

Monday morning matched my mood: overcast and dreary. I sat up and rubbed my face, already exhausted and the day hadn't begun yet. I had no idea how I was going to face Mitch and pretend I didn't know him, or that he meant nothing to me.

Because he did, regardless of how things ended.

I had fallen fast and hard. Before last night, I was certain I had found the man I wanted to spend my life with, and by every indication, he felt the same way toward me.

Except, it had been a lie. And I had lived with those long enough when I was with Jay.

I ran a weary hand through my hair and got ready for work, giving myself a pep talk the entire time. I worked in the assistant pool, helping out where needed. I spent most of my time on menial jobs, assisting other PA's with tasks, running errands, and filling in when someone was ill or on vacation. Our space was on another floor from the architects and management. I was certain that other than the occasional meeting or accidental meetup in the hall, I could avoid Mitch.

Except, when I stepped outside, he was waiting, leaning up against the outside of my building. Dressed in an overcoat that stretched across his shoulders and billowed around his knees in the breeze, he met my gaze, his expression as weary as my own.

I looked around, panicked. "What are you doing here?"

He grasped my arm, led me around the corner, and released his hold. He stood in front of me, his hands buried in his pockets. "No one from the office is going to see us, Mandy. I know you're angry with me, and you have every right to be. What I did was wrong. How I handled it was wrong. I should have said something right away—given you the choice."

"But you didn't."

"No. But I'm not giving up on us."

"There is no us."

He stepped closer. "Yes, there is. I fucked up, but I will prove it to you that you come first."

"We aren't doing this. From now on we're strangers."

His arms shot out and he tugged me close. His warmth surrounded me. He pushed my face into his chest, pressing his lips to my head. For a brief second, my pain eased with his closeness, then I pushed away.

"Stop it."

"We will never be strangers. You feel it," he challenged. "You felt how right it was for me to hold you. We'll figure this out and be together."

"We're done."

He slipped his hand under my chin, his thumb rubbing small circles on my skin. As soft as his touch was, his gaze was intense. "You go ahead and stay angry at me. I deserve it. But we're not done, and I am going to prove it to you."

His touch was so gentle, and so right. The word was out before I could stop it. "How?"

He leaned down and brushed his lips to mine. "I'll figure it out, sweetheart. When you're ready to forgive me, I'll be waiting." He stepped back. "I'll head to the office now."

"I am not riding the same bus as you." I crossed my arms, angry that he could still affect me so easily. "What were you doing at a bus stop anyway? You don't seem the sort to ride a bus."

"Another one of the many things you'll have to discover about me. I'm not a snob. I enjoy people watching and seeing the bustle around me. The city is too congested for another car, and I like the occasional bus ride. As for today, no I will not ride the bus with you. I'll grab a cab. But I had to see you before I went into the office."

"Nothing's changed."

He regarded me, not contradicting my words. "I'll see you there."

I shook my head and watched him hail a taxi and get inside. He looked over his shoulder at me, his face serious, gaze penetrating.

"You're right. Nothing has changed. I'm still crazy about you. I'll make it up, Mandy. I swear."

With those words, he disappeared.

I was on edge for the week, but nothing happened. Other PA's talked about the latest hire, but I ignored them. I heard the whispers of the hot, new consultant, and a company-wide email went out introducing Mackenzie Mitchell and his impressive resume. I stared at his picture, secretly saving it on my phone before deleting the email. It was a professional headshot, and he looked every inch the serious businessman, but the slight tilt to his lips showed his mischievous nature if you knew what to look for.

I was careful about where I went, and by the end of the week, I was convinced I could do it. Avoid Mitch and pretend the weekend never happened, and I wasn't longing to see him. The only problem was that he didn't seem to be trying as hard. Every day he sent a text.

I heard it was you who set up my office. It's perfect. Thank you.

Have a great day.

Hope you are okay.

It's raining. I hope you brought your umbrella.

I ignored them and never replied. But my day didn't feel complete until one arrived. Friday I was disappointed when one never came. I was sitting on my sofa that evening, sipping a glass of wine when my phone buzzed.

You looked pretty today.

I stared at the screen and another message popped up.

I miss you.

I responded.

***Please stop*.**

A minute went by, then two. Finally a message appeared.

Never.

I shook my head, trying not to grin. So Mitch—persistent to the end.

Saturday and Sunday, his texts were more frequent—and personal.

My bed isn't as comfortable without you in it.

My pillow smells like you.

I wish you were here.

Remember when this time last week you liked me? Can we go back to then, please?

Coffee?

Accidental run in at the market?

Meet me at the bus stop and we'll ride around for a few hours until you're not mad anymore?

Finally, Sunday night, one last one came.

Please forgive me. Give me that at least. Tell me you miss me—even a little.

I stared at the screen for a long time, then with a heavy sigh, typed a reply.

Yes.

His response was instant.

Thank you.

A while later...

My plan worked. You're talking to me again. Now, I'll move on to step 2, and yes, it's a 3 step plan.

My lips quirked, but I shut off my phone. Forgiving him was one thing, letting him get back under my skin—and into my life—another.

And neither was happening.

CHAPTER FIVE

MANDY

"Amanda."

I glanced up from the plans I was sorting and filing, forcing a smile to my face. "Hello, Michelle."

"Come with me."

I followed her, worry making me nervous. In her office, she sat, pursing her lips as she studied me. "I have a new assignment for you. Something different."

I relaxed. She hadn't found out. A new assignment I could handle.

Her next words blew that theory out of the water.

"You are going to be assisting Mr. Mack...I mean Mr. Mitchell." She allowed herself a smile. "I don't know how I mixed up his name, but I keep referring to him incorrectly. Nevertheless, he requires some help with his scheduling and office. He has agreed to your being assigned to him."

A slow burn started in my chest. I bet he did.

"Why me?" I asked through tight lips. *What had he done?*

"One of the partners suggested you. Ben Wilson told him you were invaluable last month when his PA was off ill."

"Oh."

She tilted her head. "Are you not interested? It comes with a pay increase and added benefits." She named a figure.

I had to weigh my options quickly. More money meant I could leave there sooner. Go to teacher's college. I could apply right away. If I said no, it would raise suspicion. She was already looking at me as if sensing something was off. I should be jumping at the chance, not hesitating.

But could I work with Mitch? Knowing I was going to see him, talk to him, have to face him every day? Was that part of his plan?

Michelle's eyes narrowed in suspicion. "Is there a problem, Amanda?"

"No." I shook my head. "Just an unexpected opportunity. Of course I'll help Mitch."

Her eyebrows shot up. "Mr. Mitchell."

"Oh, of-of course. Slip of the tongue."

She stood. "Don't let him catch you calling him by his first name. He is very particular about that. It's Mitchell if he allows you to be personal - not Mackenzie. Odd I know, but that is what he prefers."

"I'll keep that in mind."

Michelle knocked on Mitch's partially open door and walked in, with me trailing behind her.

"Mitchell, this is Amanda Clifford, your new PA."

He stood, rounding the desk. He held out his hand. "Amanda. What a pleasure to meet you." He folded his hand over mine, his grip too tight and too long to be professional. "May I call you Mandy?"

I glared at him, tugging back my hand. "I prefer Amanda."

He tilted his head, a smile tugging at his lips. "Funny, you look like a Mandy to me."

"You look like a Mac. But I understand you prefer Mitchell."

Michelle sucked in a horrified breath, but he threw back his head in laughter.

"I prefer Mitch to be honest, so here's the deal. Mandy and Mitch." He winked. "What a team we're going to be."

Michelle huffed and glared at me. I wanted to curse Mitch out. Her Spidey senses were tingling, and it had only been five minutes. He had just made my life harder.

"I'll leave you to it. If you need anything, *Mitchell*"—she emphasized his name—"let me know."

He leaned against his desk, crossing his ankles. "I think Mandy is going to take good care of me, Minnie. It's all good."

"Michelle. My name is Michelle."

He waved his hand. "Right. Got it. You can leave now. Shut the door behind you, please."

She stormed out, and for the first time in over a week, Mitch and I were alone with only a few feet separating us. We stared at each other. He looked tired, the sparkle I'd been drawn to missing from his eyes. I tried not to let it bother me.

"I don't know what your plan is, but we need some ground rules."

"I have no plan. I required a PA, your name came up and I agreed. I knew there was a pay increase, which would help you so I was certain you would accept. End of story."

"I call BS on that."

Mitch's eyebrows shot up and his grin was huge. His dimples stood out, and for a moment, I caught my breath at how handsome he looked. At the way he was looking at me. I shook my head.

"I'm your PA. I will assist you with your needs—your professional needs," I clarified when he grinned again. "I work for you now, so the rules of my contract must be adhered to." I paused and added quietly, "I need this job, Mitch. Don't screw this up for me."

He stood, pulling on his shirtsleeves. "I won't. I can be professional during business hours. You'll find I'm a good boss. I'm fair, courteous, respectful, and pretty laid back, despite what Monica thinks."

My lips twitched. "Michelle."

He shrugged. "She couldn't get my name right, why should I bother with hers? Might have saved me some trouble if she had."

"Are you seriously blaming her for what happened?"

He sighed. "No. But I don't like her. I don't like how she treats people. How she treats you."

"You only know that because I told you about her when I thought you were just Mitch."

He stepped closer, laying his hand on my arm. "I am Mitch. I always have been. And you're going to remember that over the next while, and we're going to move on from this."

His eyes were warm and filled with emotion. His light touch filled me with longing. I could smell his cologne. Feel his heat. Hear his desire. Feel mine begin to build.

I stepped back, breaking the spell and his hold over me.

"Let's get to work, shall we?"

For the next two weeks, Mitch proved he was a great boss. He was talented and demanding, but polite. He liked his coffee hot. Very hot. I learned once it cooled, to replace it promptly. And that he drank far too much of it. He, in turn, remembered my offhand remark about sneaking toffee, and the first day, a pretty glass dish appeared on my desk, filled with various flavors of the sweet treat. He made a big show of perching on my desk when Michelle was there and eating the candy steadily while listening to her lecture.

"I don't allow snacks at my PA's desks," she informed him.

He nodded and nonchalantly unwrapped another piece of the sticky confection. "Good thing Mandy is my PA then, isn't it, Marion?"

She stormed out. He stood, winked, and handed me a toffee.

"Carry on."

Watching him design anything was magical. Listening to him

discussing concepts and the engineering aspect of projects was sexy. He used his gorgeous hands a lot when he spoke, at times drawing in the air. I loved watching him. I had a difficult time hiding my admiration, and trying not to think of the way his hands felt on my skin.

For the first time since starting at the company, I could honestly say I enjoyed my job. He did that for me. I was challenged, busy, and appreciated. He never failed to say thank you. His smile when I would slide a fresh coffee by his elbow warmed my chest. His praise when I would assist him was heartfelt, and I found myself going above and beyond for him.

His texts still came every night. Usually, one line, but somehow he managed to express so much in them.

I love working with you.

You were amazing today. Thank you.

I love that shade of green on you. Wear it more often, okay?

I hated watching you leave today. Monday seems too far away.

I miss you, Mandy. Tell me you want to figure this out. Please, sweetheart.

Memories of our time played through my mind. His words, his humor, the way he touched me—the explosive passion we had together. If I were being honest, I hated leaving him too. But there was so much at stake. I needed my job. I had to decide if I could trust him again.

I didn't reply to his message.

Mitch looked tired all week, and on Thursday, he was hit with a deadline and a design change he hadn't expected. He worked all day, barely leaving his desk. Around seven, I went into his office and slid a coffee by his elbow. He glanced up, startled.

"I thought you had left."

"No. I wanted to stay and see if I could help."

He picked up the coffee and sipped. "This helps."

"Good. I got some sandwiches."

He captured my hand and squeezed it. "Thank you." He looked toward the sofa. "Eat with me? I need the distraction."

"Okay."

He devoured the simple meal I brought him while I nibbled. He sat back, draining the soda, and wiping his mouth.

"Thanks, sweetheart."

My soda froze part way to my mouth. He shut his eyes with a sigh.

"Sorry. Thanks, Mandy."

I focused my eyes on the floor. It had felt so good to hear him call me sweetheart.

"It's fine," I mumbled.

"It's how I think of you all the time. My Mandy. My sweetheart."

I glanced up, my fingers playing with the edge of my skirt. "You think of me?"

"Every damn minute of every damn day—and night."

Our gazes locked. He leaned closer. "You're the first thing I think of when I wake up, and the last thing on my mind when I go to sleep." He snorted. "If I sleep."

"Why aren't you sleeping?" I whispered. I knew why I was having trouble finding rest.

"Because all I can think about is if I had been honest from the get-go and confessed who I was and that I would be working here, we could have figured this out together. The instant chemistry between us was too hot to have been denied and I knew we would have come up with something. Instead, I tried to buy myself some time. Stupid move on my part." He ran a hand through his hair. "I never thought how it might affect you, job-wise. I'm sorry for that. For all of it, actually."

He stood with a defeated smile. "At least I get to see you every day. Talk to you." He lifted his shoulder. "Hear you laugh. I love your laugh. It helps me get through the day."

He gazed down at me. "Maybe one day you can forgive me. Maybe one day this place won't stand between us. That is my greatest hope."

His sincerity was real. His expression honest and sad. The words were out of my mouth before I could stop them.

"I miss you too. Promise me you will never lie to me again."

"Never."

"I forgive you."

He was on me in a second, his body pressing me into the cushions of the sofa, his mouth hungry and demanding. His arms were like vises around my body, holding me tight. He devoured me. Surrounded by his body, his taste and scent soaking into me, I finally felt right again.

He was right.

We were right.

And I was tired of denying it.

He dragged his lips across my cheek. "Sweetheart, I need to take you home."

"You have work to do and a deadline."

"The only thing I want to work on is getting inside you," he protested.

"You have a building to create."

"I've got something else erected instead," he insisted with a grin, flexing his hips and grinding into me.

I moaned low in my throat. "Mitch, please. We can't. Not here."

Before he could speak, a cold voice startled us.

"Well, isn't this cozy? I knew something was going on."

Michelle stood in the doorway, her arms crossed.

I stared at the wall, gripping the hot cup of tea Mitch had given me. I shivered a little, pulling the blanket Mitch had draped around my shoulders tighter. I could hear his voice in the other room, talking on the phone with his lawyer.

When Michelle discovered us, Mitch had stood, angry and indignant.

"Does a closed door mean anything to you?"

She shook her head. "Stop deflecting." She glared at me. "You're in breach of contract. You're fired."

Mitch laid a hand on my shoulder. "You fire her, I'll walk."

She rolled her eyes. "Take it up with management."

He met her gaze steadily. "Trust me, I will. Now, get out of my office."

After she flounced out, he picked up his phone and jacket. "Get your things. We're leaving."

"Your deadline..." I protested.

He leaned over me. "Fuck that. Fuck everything but fixing this for you. Sweetheart, I'm so sorry."

"For kissing me?"

He stroked my cheek. "Never. But I should have waited until we were out of the office. I messed up, but I promise I will fix it."

His tone was serious, his expression sincere.

"Okay."

"You trust me?"

"Yes."

He kissed me. "That's all I need to know. Now, let me get you out of here."

He strode in the room, tossing down the phone and kissing me.

"Good news or bad?" he asked.

"Bad first."

"You're fired."

"Hardly a surprise. What's the good news?"

"I got you a new job. A much better one."

"Oh?"

He grinned and sat beside me, rubbing my legs. "Several years ago, my lawyer added a clause in my contract I've never used and had forgotten about."

"Which is?"

"It's long and technical, but basically, if I don't like the PA the company provides for me, I can hire my own." He smirked. "You take orders from me now, not that cow Michelle. You are my direct employee." He winked. "And unlike Parson's—I highly encourage fraternization."

My eyebrows shot up. "*What*? But what if they don't agree to your choice?"

He shrugged, confident. "They will. I told them it was that, or I was gone. I have a thirty-day departure clause in my contract and I will use it."

"But, your career—your reputation," I protested. "You signed a lease for this place—you just moved here for this job!"

He tilted his head with a frown. "This place, my job, is nothing compared to how this affects you. Us. That's the important thing here, Mandy." He brushed a piece of hair off my cheek. "I'm putting you first. Us first."

I gripped his wrist. "But—"

He shook his head. "No buts. You. First."

"Why?" I asked, my throat tight.

"It's a job. I'll get another one if it comes down to that. And I don't give a flying fuck about my reputation. Frankly, I'm sought-after enough that I don't care. What I do care about is making sure you're okay, and that we can be together." He kissed me. "All of that is noise, Mandy. What I feel for you, what I think is happening between us—that's what's real. What is important."

I blinked at him. "I think—I think I'm falling in love with you, Mitch."

He tapped his head. "Good. Then my plan has worked. Because as crazy as it sounds, I'm already in love with you."

"Slowing your roll, I see."

He winked. "You know it."

He cupped my face. "I'm making you a promise right now. Honesty and you first. Always."

I smiled through my tears.

"So, Amanda Clifford, with the sexy legs and wickedly talented mouth that can whistle like nobody's business...among other things." He paused with a sly grin, "Are you ready to come work for me, be my girlfriend, and let me kiss that gifted mouth of yours any time I want?"

"Is that considered a benefit?"

"Absolutely."

"Is it a term contract?"

He shook his head. "Perpetual."

"Okay, then."

"Yeah?" The dimples I loved popped. His smile was huge, but it was the expression in his eyes that struck me. Earnest, yearning, and determined. I knew, at that moment, I was making the right decision.

"I accept."

He leaned down and kissed me. "Thank you, sweetheart, for trusting me. I won't let you down again. We're going to make the best team—ever."

And as I kissed him back, I knew he was right.

EPILOGUE

Step 1

Mandy

I glanced around the empty space, trying to envision what Mitch had planned. The soaring ceilings, exposed beams, and skylights made the large square footage bright and open, but it was in such disrepair, I couldn't see beyond the piles of discarded garbage, dust and cobwebs, and especially the cooing of the pigeons that had nested in the high beams.

Mitch came around the corner, beaming. "Well, sweetheart? What do you think?"

"Ah..." I hesitated. "It's so...ah, dirty?"

He threw back his head in laughter and caught me in his arms. "It's filthy. Disgusting, really."

I pursed my lips. "And we like disgusting now?"

"No, but it works well for negotiations. I can see the potential here." He turned me in his embrace, sweeping out his arm. "I'll hire a company to come in and clean. Remove the critters and detox the place. Downstairs will be reception and offices. Work spaces. Up here is all mine." He dropped a kiss to my neck, his lips warm on my skin. "*Ours*. I'll create a beautiful space for you to work in beside me. The center will be a huge table—a living edge one—with space to meet clients or work at. My area will be along the back by those windows. Light," he sighed in happiness. "So much light."

I folded my hands over his, squeezing them affectionately. "Tell me more."

"A kitchen over there so you can make me sandwiches. A private bathroom with a stand-up, multiheaded shower I can fuck you in. A big comfy sofa I can work on when I'm sketching and I can nap with you on when I need to recharge, a—"

My laugh cut him off. "This is supposed to be an office, Mitch. You're planning a lot of personal stuff in here."

He drew me closer. "I am. You'll be with me, so it's a given. This will be ours, Mandy. Our little empire. I won't answer to anyone anymore, and you will never have to deal with the likes of Michelle again."

I sighed as I leaned back into his chest. His chin rested on my shoulder as we both studied the empty shell of the building Mitch wanted to purchase and open his own company.

"I want to hire the best and brightest. Create a positive space where my architects and designers can thrive. Work with people equally as passionate as I am," he mused. "And with you by my side, I can do that."

I nodded, beginning to see his vision. Once cleaned and rebuilt to his specifications, the space would be amazing. Clean lines, modern touches, and his design would have clients flocking in. There were already phone calls and inquiries about the rumors of his new venture.

I thought back to the last year of our life.

Returning to Parson Planners as Mitch's employee had been a nerve-racking, stressful time at first. Walking through the doors beside him, I felt the resentful stares and, over the next while, discovered the people who were real as opposed to the ones who were spiteful and catty. I heard the gossip and witnessed the way conversation would cease when I entered the kitchen to get Mitch one of his endless cups of coffee. I did my best to ignore it, although at times it overwhelmed me. A few women showed their merit by treating me no differently, even going so far as to nudge my shoulder and wish me a whispered congrats on snagging the hottie. When I realized they were teasing and genuinely happy for me, I was able to relax and concentrate on my job.

Mitch never faltered. The first day, he had stopped outside and turned to me, his usually teasing smile absent.

"Keep your head up and be proud, Mandy. We haven't done anything wrong. Don't let anyone make you think we have. Nothing has changed except you have a far better pay grade and your new boss appreciates you. Understand?"

I squared my shoulders. "Got it."

Each day, he was driven and passionate. He worked hard, and I loved being part of his creative projects. He was professional at all times, never displaying over-the-top PDA or drawing attention to the fact that we were a couple, but he was vigilant and fast to shut things down if he heard unkind remarks or witnessed something that displeased him. He was protective and strong but allowed me to find my own path in the office, which I appreciated. I knew he didn't care, and if he had his way, he would demonstrate his affection openly, but he toned it down for my sake.

Behind closed doors was a different story. He often kissed my cheek, trailed his fingers down my face, touched my arm or hand while we were working, and his praise was lavish. His good-morning kiss was long and deep, and I learned not to bother with lipstick until after it happened. Regardless of the fact that we might have spent the night together, or even arrived at the office hand in hand until we entered the building, he refused to start his day without his kiss.

"I have to hold back for ten hours," he grouched when I told him he was being silly.

"I am here all day. You see me all day," I stressed. "You even kiss me at times."

"Not like this," he had countered, sweeping me into his arms and covering my mouth with his. I forgot about the office or anything else when his tongue slid along mine, sensuous and wicked. He kissed me until I was breathless and trembling in his embrace, then released me.

"That is how I want to start my day," he insisted. "After that, I'll be your boss. But until that very second, I'm your Mitch, and you're my sweetheart. Got it?"

I lifted a trembling hand to my mouth, feeling his possession.

"Okay," I whispered.

He dropped another kiss to my lips with a grin. "I'll dial it back a bit, Mandy. I don't want you distracted and eyeing me in an unprofessional manner, now do I?" He winked with a leer.

I had to laugh. "Heaven forbid."

I had feared Michelle would be the hardest to deal with, and I was right. I had just refilled my pretty bowl of toffees, which I'd found upside down in the garbage can, when she stormed in, her face like thunder. Mitch appeared instantly, standing beside me.

She placed a pile of paperwork on my desk, which was empty except for my candy dish.

She stated that, given I was now Mitch's employee, my computer and supplies would be provided by him, and I was not at liberty to remove office supplies. Anything I used would be charged to Mitch. He had perched casually on the edge of my desk, snagging toffees and opening them with gusto, humming over their flavor and forcing me to hide my grin at his actions. He interrupted her tirade.

"What does a stapler go for these days, Mildred? A good quality one. I like a good, solid stapler."

She frowned, perplexed. "I have no idea. And it's Michelle."

He rubbed his chin. "Any thoughts on paper clips? I like those plastic-coated ones—the kind that don't leave rust spots if you spill something on them."

She shook her head, unsure if he was being serious. I was trying my best not to laugh.

"Huh." He shrugged. "I thought you'd be more up-to-date on supply costs, Milly. They certainly seem like a priority to you."

He unwrapped another candy and handed it to me. "Your favorite," he said with a wink. "Be sure to order more of these, okay? And get a dish for my desk too. On my bill, of course."

"Of course," I murmured, my lips twitching.

Michelle tapped the paperwork. "These forms must be filled out immediately. If they aren't completed today, there will be consequences."

I resisted the urge to roll my eyes.

Mitch nodded and patted his pockets with a frown.

"Okay, I'll get Mandy on those straightaway. You got a pen, Matilda? We seem to be out."

"No," she snapped.

Then she went over rules and regulations, office etiquette, and guidelines—and informed me, in no uncertain terms, I was no longer an employee of Parson Planners, therefore no longer had access to the staff lounge or the perks of being a staff member.

"Don't overstep your position." She sniffed, glaring at me. "You have lost all your privileges here with your foolish behavior."

I saw Mitch's shoulders tense, and I knew she had crossed the line.

He stood, smoothing down his tie and tilting his head.

"How old do you think I am, Michelle?" he asked, cold and clipped.

Internally I grimaced. He had never called her by her proper name or in that tone of voice.

She huffed out a sigh. "I am aware of your age, Mitch."

He shook his head. "Then cease speaking to Mandy and me as if we were twelve and under your control. Frankly, the way you've just outlined the structure, I feel as if I'm simply renting space here instead of being part of the team the way I have been the past while. I'm not sure I welcome that feeling." He held up his hand as she began to speak. "No. It's my turn to talk. If Mandy is being treated as an outsider, then I will be as well since she's a huge part of my operation now. So that being said, I expect you to follow these rules."

He stepped forward. "I will discuss this inane rule of supplies with Mr. Parson, and we will come to an agreement. I think you're forgetting your place here, madam. I don't work for you in any capacity. The way it was outlined to me, you are here to make sure things run smoothly for me if necessary. I don't consider your bitchy attitude to be helpful in the least. In fact, it adds a level of stress to my workday I don't appreciate. I'll be sure to address this with the partners when I speak with them later."

Her mouth opened, but nothing came out. He continued.

"You will address me as Mr. Mitchell. Not Mackenzie and certainly not Mitch. You will speak to Mandy about business items only, and you will treat her with the same respect you would any other person in this building. More so, in fact. You will refrain from discussing me or her with anyone. If I hear otherwise, I'll go straight to the partners and address my concerns, and my lawyer will be involved. Do you understand me?"

Their furious gazes locked in a battle of wills. She broke first, casting her eyes downward. "Yes," she huffed out. She tapped the paperwork, addressing me. "Read through these files, sign where indicated, and return them to my office." She swallowed, the next word ripped from her throat as if it killed her to utter it. "Please."

"I'll have them to you by the end of the day."

She turned and marched to the door.

"One more thing, Michelle." Mitch emphasized her name so she knew he was serious.

"And that is?"

"You will knock before entering this office. Every. Damn. Time. Do I make myself clear?"

If looks could kill, he'd be dead on the floor. As it was, he appeared cool and unaffected by her anger. On the other hand, I was a shaking mess, unsure what was going to happen next.

"Crystal," she snapped and stormed out, the door shutting too loudly to be considered polite.

He studied the door, then swung around. "Well, that's handled. Let's go to the supply room and get your stuff back."

"But she just said..."

He leaned on the desk. "Fuck her. I already knew there was going to be trouble with her, and I'm prepared for it. Your things are in a box in the supply cabinet, and I'm going to go get them and you can set up your desk again and order anything else you need. I'll be billed through the company, the way my contract outlined it, but the basics are part of the deal. She took your stuff to be a bitch—nothing more." He snorted. "She didn't think I'd call her on it. If she thinks I don't know what I'm doing, she's got it all wrong. I'll wipe the floor with her."

I stared up at him, speechless, and he leaned close, cupping my cheek. "If she so much as breathes in your direction, I want to know about it, you understand? You work for me, and you are under my protection. She has zero control over you."

"Okay."

"We need to get you a new computer. You'll have access to their drive, but I want all my work on machines I own. The same as yours. That was nonnegotiable when I spoke with them."

"You went to a lot of trouble over this. Over me."

He stood, pulling me to my feet in a tight hug. "And you're worth it. First, remember?"

He had never wavered from those words. But as his time with Parson Planners went by, he decided two things: he liked Toronto and wanted to stay, but he no longer wanted to work for anyone but himself. The year had been fraught with tension due to Michelle and his constant clashes with one of the partners who felt Mitch wasn't giving them his best, even though the rest of the people involved in the project disagreed. He made life difficult for both Mitch and me whenever he could, and Mitch had been perplexed until the night we saw him and Michelle out at dinner, acting like anything but coworkers. They tried to convince him there was nothing going on, but he had laughed at them, now understanding the hostility. He couldn't be bothered, and he didn't care what they did outside of office hours, but he let them stew over it.

Mitch had reached his limit.

So here we were.

"Are you really doing this?" I asked. "You have so many offers. You always liked having someone else manage the people, while you looked after the design."

He pressed a kiss to my head and walked around, lost in his thoughts. He turned, studying me across the large room.

"You're right, I did. But things changed this past year. I saw what happens when a place is badly run. How morale can suffer. I also saw how being treated well can change an employee's outlook on their job. Their loyalty. I don't want to give anyone else the opportunity to tell me how to live my life—or who I can love." He ran a hand through his hair. "I'll be a good boss. I don't have to give up what I do. I'll have you, and we'll hire a good office manager. Someone who treats the staff well. With my reputation, and the people I'm going to hire, we'll put this place on the map in no time."

"I know you will," I assured him.

He grinned. "All the people coming to me with job offers right now can hire my company. They'll get the whole experience."

I eyed the space. "Um, how long until you think that will happen?"

"This is step one. I'm putting in the offer today. I've already got a contractor in mind, and we'll start right away. I can work from home or a rented space. Anyone I hire can do the same. That part is easy. I think we'll be in the space in about six months, and until then, we'll find a spot we can meet. With the internet I can meet with anyone, anytime at the touch of a button. Our last day with Parson's is in two weeks. As soon as we are done, MM Designs is full steam ahead."

I smiled. "Step one? Got another three-step plan going on?"

He chuckled. "Yep."

I beamed at him. "I'm so proud of you, Mitch."

He crossed the room, taking my hand. "There's another reason, Mandy."

"Oh?"

"Toronto is your home, and you love it here. I love it here. I want to build my life with you, so this is the place it's going to happen. We'll start with the company and then we'll build our life together."

"I like the sound of that."

He huffed out a long breath and played with my fingers. He was serious and edgy—a mood I didn't often see with Mitch.

"What is it?"

"I want something, Mandy. Something only you can give me."

His voice made me nervous. I tried to make him smile.

"A blow job? Now?" I looked around. "I'd prefer to wait until I don't have to be worried about being pooped on by pigeons, but if you insist..." I shrugged.

He threw back his head in laughter and hugged me fast. "I'll take you up on that later."

I giggled. "What do you want then?"

"I want to buy a place to live."

"Oh. Move out of your rented place?"

"Yes."

"Okay. And you need my help to find a place?"

He slid his hand up my arm and around the back of my neck. "I want you to choose the place, because I want you to live there with me."

"You-you want me to move in with you?" I sputtered. He had hinted often, but he'd never come right out and said so until now.

"I want more than that, but it's a good start."

"More?" I repeated.

"I want to marry you. Have kids. Holidays. Memories. Grandkids. I want all of it with you."

I could only mouth the word *wow*.

He gripped my neck, pulling me close and resting his forehead to mine. "I'm trying to slow my roll here, Mandy, but you need to know the whole picture. I know it's too much to ask right now, but please think about moving in with me. I want you with me all the time. Here at the office. Beside me at home. Asleep next to me at night. Please come and live with me."

"Okay."

"Okay, you'll think about it, or okay, you will?"

I paused, unsure which one I meant. Then I realized how stupid I was being. I loved Mitch. He loved me. I had never known the sort of love he offered me on a daily basis. Freely given and complete. I wanted to be with him as well.

"Okay, I will," I responded.

He swung me into his arms, his mouth hard on mine. He kissed me until I was breathless, light-headed, and aching for him. He set me on my feet, cupping my face and raining small kisses on my face.

"My sweetheart," he breathed. "My Mandy."

Then he grinned. "Wait until I tell them."

"Them?"

His grin widened, his eyes dancing with mischievousness. His dimples were so deep I could stick the end of my finger in them.

"I had Mom, Kris, and Joseph ready to send you their top ten reasons why you should live with me. Mom actually has a Power Point presentation ready if you needed extra persuasion, and Kris said she wasn't above bribery."

I started to laugh. "Another three-step plan, Mitch?"

"They worked in the past. I was going with proven results."

I cupped his cheek. "No need. I love you, and I want to be with you too."

He turned his face and kissed my palm.

"Then let's go celebrate."

Another Year Later

Step 2

The office buzzed around me as I worked on Mitch's calendar. Since opening MM Designs, he had been in high demand. So much so, there was a waiting list. The other architects he hired worked with him on several of the projects, helping ease some of the burden, but it was Mackenzie Mitchell's name they wanted. His designs. His signature on the plans.

He was amazing.

I rolled my shoulders, frowning as I looked at his schedule. He was going to be away a lot over the next few months. Site visits, openings, meetings. I hated it when he went away, but it was part of the job. He refused to hand over some things, and I understood. His visions, his reputation—both were too important to him.

I lifted my mug, not surprised to find my coffee had gone cold. I strolled to the kitchen, deciding a fresh Nespresso was in order. Mitch had gotten me addicted to them.

As the coffee brewed, I wandered over to the open space in the middle of the office. Mitch had made a cutout in the center of the floor, right down to the main level. Sunlight from the skylights filtered down, making every floor airy and bright. On hot days, a special canopy covered the roof, allowing some light to filter in but blocking the heat. Custom-made clear boxes held models of Mitch's buildings displayed at different heights, showing off his work. It was quite breathtaking.

Looking over the glass rail, I admired all the space below. Everyone was busy. Everyone was happy. Mitch held true to his word of providing a positive environment for everyone to work in. The two floors below us had work spaces and private offices for architects and designers. The main floor was accounting, production, and a huge staff room. He'd had a gym built in the basement that everyone had access to. It was a great place to work.

The third floor was entirely Mitch's, except for the large boardroom where everyone gathered for meetings or to celebrate the latest contract or completion of a project.

I heard the beep of the machine and crossed back to the kitchen to get my coffee. I sat at my desk, smiling as I heard the private elevator door open. It came up from the parking lot, and the only person with access to it was Mitch.

He strode in, cardboard tubes under his arm, a wide smile on his face, and a huge bunch of flowers gripped in his free hand.

He saw me, and his smile became wider. His dimples deepened and his eyes crinkled. With a flourish, he presented me with the flowers.

"For you, sweetheart."

"They loved the design?"

He winked. "As if there was any doubt. Signed, sealed, and delivered."

I leaned close and brushed a kiss to his lips. "Congratulations, Mitch."

He wound his arm around my waist, yanking me tight and kissing me with passion. He swept his tongue into my mouth with a low groan and wrapped his hand around my neck, keeping me close.

I was almost panting by the time he finished.

"Um, wow?" I whispered.

"This is the one, sweetheart. It will make the company number one. I know it. We won't be able to keep up."

I chuckled, wiping my gloss from his mouth. "We're already having trouble with that. If you took on every project you were offered, I wouldn't see you for three years."

He tapped the end of my nose affectionately. "That will never do."

He leaned across me, picking up my coffee and taking a long drink.

"Hey! That was mine."

"I know. I love drinking from your cup. Your lips add an extra flavor to it."

I rolled my eyes. "You are such a dork."

"Romantic. You're always mixing up your words, Mandy. I'm romantic."

"Whatever."

He studied me, then with a wink, took another long sip.

"I'm thinking of opening a second office."

"Here?"

"No. I was thinking overseas—Sweden. We're getting so many tender bids over there. I would prefer to have an office to work from—a central location."

My heart sank. If Mitch opened another office overseas, he'd be away more. I'd hardly ever see him. But I forced a smile to my face.

"That will be interesting."

His phone rang, but he ignored it. His eyes searched my face, and he frowned. "What is it?"

I waved my hand. "Nothing. You just surprised me. I'm sure it would be amazing."

His phone rang again, and he dug into his pocket. "Shit, I need to take this."

I made my voice sound chipper. "Enough flirting with your staff, Mr. Mitchell. Get back to work. I'm going to put these flowers in water and make you your own coffee."

I slid past him as he answered his phone, not meeting his eyes. I needed to process so I could support him.

But the question kept returning.

What about me? What about us?

Mitch

I glanced up from my drafting table, stretching my arms. It was later than I thought. The sun had set, the automatic lighting already on. I had been so lost in my vision, I hadn't even noticed. I bent sideways, peering into the outer office. Mandy's desk was empty, but I knew she was around. I crossed the office, stopping by the heavy glass door that gave me privacy and the quiet I needed to concentrate but allowed me to see everything happening when I wanted to, and located Mandy. She was on the huge sectional sofa, sorting papers on the coffee table. I held back my smile, knowing she was working on my expense report. Once she was done, I would have to take her to dinner to say thanks.

I was awful at keeping track of my expenditures. Mandy had full access to my credit cards and tried to keep up, digging through my pockets and wallet to find the receipts I forgot to drop into the box she kept for them. Whenever possible, I had the receipt emailed, but I was a fail at that a great deal of the time as well.

I studied her as she bent over the table. She had pulled her hair up and had removed her jacket, her soft silk blouse showing off her arms and delicate neck. She had kicked off her shoes, the high heels she hated but wore because she knew how much I loved how sexy they made her legs look. She was muttering, biting her lip in frustration, and I cracked the door a little, listening to her utter my name along with a few choice curse words. She was adorable.

She also looked tired—more than usual. I knew I kept her busy, both here and at home. I had been away a lot—more than I'd planned or wanted to be. She hated it, although she never complained. The sadness on her face when I would leave said it all.

She had been restless the past few nights, and twice I had woken to find her on the sofa, curled up with a blanket. I was sure she had been crying, but she insisted everything was fine.

"I just wandered out for a drink of water and passed out on the sofa," she laughed, waving my worry away. "You know I do that on occasion."

She did, but usually there was a glass as evidence. I needed to figure out what was going on with her.

I pulled open the door, and she looked up with a smile.

"All done?"

I dropped a kiss to her head and flung myself onto the sofa close to her. "For now." I scrubbed my face. "Am I safe to be in the same room as you?"

She laughed, securing some slips of paper into place. "I have most of it. You were so busy last month, there are a lot of receipts. I'll find the rest tomorrow." She flashed me a smile, but it seemed forced. "But you owe me dinner."

"I owe you a lot more than that."

"We can start with food."

I leaned back on the sofa, studying her as she gathered all the bits of paper that took me away from her. Cabs, meals, plane tickets, hotel bills. And there would be more in the next while. It hit me right then what was going on.

I was an idiot.

At the office, Mandy was so good at reading me that sometimes I didn't have to complete my thoughts—she simply knew what I was going to say, or anticipated my needs and acted accordingly.

But at times, on a personal level, she needed more. And I had neglected that part of our relationship this week, dropping a bombshell on her without following up later at home.

"How about we start with a little clarification?" I mused, draping my arms over the back of the sofa.

She slid the lid onto the receipt box. "About?"

I tilted my head. "I love you, Mandy."

Her smile was genuine this time. "I love you too, Mitch."

"You are my nucleus, sweetheart. Everything I've accomplished, every step of my plan, I can't possibly do without you."

"Oh." She seemed confused. "Well, I'm right here."

"I know. I said something the other day, and I didn't say it properly."

She swallowed, her throat working nervously. "And?"

"I told you I want to maybe open up another office. But what I didn't say was if I did, whenever I go, I plan to take you with me. In fact, I want you to start traveling with me as much as possible."

"You-you do?"

I held out my hand, and she let me pull her across the sofa. She straddled my lap, her skirt riding up, the lace of her thigh-highs peeking out from under the material.

For a moment, I was distracted, rubbing the rough texture between my fingers.

"Jesus," I muttered. "You've been wearing these all day?"

She slapped my hands. "Yes."

Sliding my hands up her legs, I gripped her hips, trying not to notice the way she was nestled right against my cock. Or the fact that he noticed it too and wanted her a little closer.

I met her worried gaze.

"Mandy, sweetheart, you are one of the most intelligent, organized women I have ever met. The way you run this office—run me—is nothing short of a miracle. You know me so well." I pulled her face close to mine, leaning my forehead against hers. "How can you not know how much I need you with me as much as possible?"

"I rarely come with you on your trips."

"Because they're usually overnight, filled with meetings, and boring as shit. I know you hate to fly, and I don't want you tense all the time. Knowing you're here when I get back, the office is running smoothly, your beautiful smile is waiting for me, helps me so much. But, baby, I would never go away for a long period and not ask you to go with me." I cupped her cheeks and made her meet my eyes. "Ever."

"Yeah?" she questioned, worry in her gaze.

"Yeah. And when I said open another office, I meant using my name, hiring the best and overseeing it—mostly from here. There's an architect in Sweden I've been in contact with. Young, brilliant—I think he'll do great things. I would take some trips there, but with the technology we have, I am in the office there in seconds with the push of a button." I stroked her cheek. "I didn't plan on being gone without you for weeks at a time."

She sighed, the sound low and quivering. That was exactly what she had thought.

"Baby, you know me better than that."

"It's just, you've been so busy, so in your element and...happy. I thought-I thought—" she shrugged "—I don't know what I thought."

"I am happy, but only because I love this place and I have you. Especially the fact that I have you. You first, remember?"

Tears filled her eyes and I kissed them away. "I'm sorry, sweetheart. I made you doubt that. I've been taking you for granted, haven't I?"

"No." She shook her head, but I silenced her.

"I have. You're so amazing, and I forget to tell you that. But I'll do better. I know you trust Lauren—do you think she could oversee the office if we were both gone on occasion?"

"I think so. The rest of the office is a breeze compared to running you."

With a chuckle, I kissed her. "Then you can come with me when I head over to Sweden. Any trip over three days, you come with me."

She fiddled with my tie. "Anything over a week." She met my surprised gaze. "You do a lot of three-day trips." Her eyes slid to the side, and a smile tugged on her lips. "I don't mind the break."

I burst out laughing. "Done."

"You really want me with you?"

I slid my hand around the back of her neck. "I always want you with me, Mandy. I do better when you're close. We're a great team."

"Is overseas step two of your plan?"

"Yep."

"What is step three?"

"Getting my business so successful, I can cut back, marry you, knock you up with lots of babies, and enjoy life with you."

"Um, I think you're already successful. I saw your bank account the other day. The number of zeros is frightening."

"Then we can move to step three soon." I pulled her face close. "In fact, maybe we should practice."

"Here?"

"Right here. Right now." I widened my legs so she slid down against me, the warmth of her pressing on my cock. "I want you to ride me on this sofa, Mandy."

"Is that Mackenzie talking or Mitch?"

I grinned. "They're both horny bastards in love with their assistant. So, whoever you want—he's yours."

She pressed close, her mouth hovering over mine.

"Mitch," she breathed out. "I want my Mitch."

"Done," I growled, yanking her face to mine and kissing her with utter abandon. She was sweet under my tongue—toffee and Mandy, the very best combination. She moaned low in her throat as I ran my fingers up her sides, cupping her breasts.

I dragged my mouth across her cheek, down her neck, swirling and tasting her skin, smiling at the shivers racing down her spine.

"I'm sorry," I whispered into her ear.

"For wh—"

I hooked my fingers into the neckline of her blouse and yanked. The material gave away easily under my fists, exposing her pretty lingerie. Ivory lace, satin ribbons, and pink bows made me groan.

"It's amazing I get any work done, wondering what you have on under your clothes."

"I liked that blouse!" she gasped.

"I'll buy you another one." One flick of my wrist and her breasts spilled into my hands. I licked and sucked on her buds until they were hard and wet, and her breathing fast. I slid my hands along the backs of her thighs, pushing up her skirt. "What are you hiding here, Mandy? More lace? More satin?"

She arched her eyebrow, teasing and pleased with herself. I soon discovered why.

All my fingers encountered was skin. Soft, silky skin.

"Jesus. You've been bare. All fucking day, you've been bare."

She moaned as I delved between her legs, finding her slick and ready.

"Does someone want to be fucked?" I licked at the shell of her ear. "Tell me."

Her nimble fingers pulled at my belt, yanked on my zipper, and tugged on my pants. "Hips up," she instructed, her voice quivering with need.

I lifted my hips, and in seconds, my pants were at my ankles, my erection between us, hard and straining.

She braced herself on the cushion behind my head, the action pushing her breast right into my mouth. I groaned around her nipple as she sank down on me, inch by inch until she was full. Until we were flush. Then she leaned back, the action taking me deeper.

"Mandy," I moaned, the feeling intense.

She grasped my chin, her eyes wild. "Yes, Mitch. The answer is yes. I want to be fucked."

I grasped her hips and bucked. Her eyes rolled back in her head, and she gripped my shoulders. "More."

I gave her more. I gave her all I had. Thrusting. Straining. Pounding into her. Sweat beaded on my forehead, and my back grew damp. With a curse, I stood, still inside her, and laid her on the sofa, bracing myself above her. I lifted one of her legs over my shoulder, smiling as she gasped at the angle and how deep I was seated inside. I took her hard, mindless of anything but the pleasure being inside her gave me. I grunted. Groaned. Panted. Snarled in passion. Whispered in adoration. She mewled and whimpered, her voice keening my name.

"Give it to me, Mandy. Come for me," I begged, feeling my balls begin to tighten and the ecstasy wind itself around my spine.

She stiffened, her pussy contracting around me, hot, wet, taking all I had. My orgasm hit me, obliterating everything in its path. I shouted, cursed, and shook. Then collapsed, mindless, my legs no longer able to hold me up.

I pulled Mandy closer, kissing her forehead. After I had recovered, I moved us both onto the sofa, wrapping us in the cashmere blanket, still too lazy to move very far.

"You know, when I looked at this place, I asked you something."

"Hmm," she agreed, sleepy and sated. "You hinted at a blow job, then asked me to move in with you."

I chuckled at her memory. "I settled for that, but I wanted something else."

She lifted her head with a frown.

"You did?"

"I told you I wanted you to marry me."

With a soft smile, she rubbed her cheek on my hand. "Yes, you did."

I nestled my chin on her neck. "Well?"

"Is that a proposal?"

I chuckled. "That's a what-if. If I asked you that question, would you say yes now?"

"If I were dressed, holding a glass of champagne, and convinced the question wasn't orgasm-induced, then your chances are looking good."

I kissed her, already making plans.

"Okay then, Mandy. Prepare yourself."

Step 3

Mandy

I sat back and looked at all the parcels on the back seat of the limo with me, still a little confused. Mitch had sent me out on endless errands, and I had been gone all afternoon. It was unusual he asked me to go shopping for him or to pick up things outside the office. He had always insisted I have one of the other junior assistants do any task of that sort, but today he had been very insistent it was me who had to go and pick up various items for him. I had been to the pharmacist, the post office, picked up three different packages at exclusive stores I had never heard of, and a final stop at the bakery. Everywhere I went, the items were ready for me. I had no clue what was in the boxes and bags, although I was sure I would find out. I'd carry them to the car he had hired to drive me everywhere, then move on to the next item on the list. I slid my phone from my pocket to send him a message. I typed it out with a grin.

I feel like a drug mule. So many mysterious packages.

His reply made me laugh.

Drug mules carry drugs across borders, sweetheart. I'm local. And the only drug I'm hooked on is you.

I replied.

What do you call all these errands?

His reply was typical Mitch.

Taking care of your man. You will be amply rewarded.

I smirked as I shot back a retort.

I had better be.

He sent one last text.

Open the small box from the bakery. That will keep you going and start your rewards.

A simple vanilla cupcake piled high with frosting waited for me in the box. A napkin was tucked along the side. With a happy sigh, I leaned back into the luxurious leather upholstery and bit into the rich cake. He knew me so well. I sent him back a row of kisses, knowing he wouldn't reply. He would know the cupcake had all my attention now.

I watched the traffic around us, the car crawling slowly back toward the office. I was sure Mitch would explain why it was me he had sent out today. He would open the parcels and boxes and show me everything, and it would all make sense. He had been unusually quiet the last few days, constantly on his phone, shut away in his office, and working late—sending me home without him. He said he had a big project on the go and didn't want to say anything until it was confirmed. It was the first time he hadn't shared with me, and I didn't like it, although I had to respect his decision. It had to be huge for him not to talk to me about it, because Mitch talked to me about everything. Maybe tonight I could get him to open up. I looked at the frosting on the last bite of cake before I popped it into my mouth.

I knew exactly how to get him to open up. I only hoped the larger box contained more cupcakes.

The office was quiet when I stepped off the elevator, balancing the large box from the bakery and a couple of bags in my hands. The driver walked past me, setting the various boxes and bags on the table and floor. He winked as he returned to the elevator, tipping his hat.

"Have a pleasant evening, ma'am."

"Wait, I haven't—"

He held up his hand, cutting me off. "All been taken care of." He smiled. "All the best."

His last words confused me, but I crossed the office toward my desk. I realized how low the lights were and how quiet the building seemed. I glanced toward the clock with a frown. It was only just past five. Normally the office was buzzing until six—often well past. I slid the box onto my desk and set the bags on the floor. With a start, I saw Mitch standing at the center of the office, staring over the railing, seemingly lost in thought. He had changed, his navy suit hugging his shoulders, tailored and smart. It was my favorite.

"Mitch?" I called.

He turned with a smile, holding out his hand. "Hey, sweetheart, you're back."

Something in his voice made me tense. Mitch was always calm, confident, and sure. There was an edge to his tone—one I wasn't used to hearing. I hurried toward him, letting him take my hand and pull me close.

"Are you all right?" I asked, concerned. I cupped his cheek. "Did you get some bad news on your project? What can I do to help?"

His eyes were warm and tender as he smiled at me. "Always worried about me, aren't you, Mandy? Always wanting to help me." He tilted his head. "It's one of the things I love so much about you. The *way* you love me." He inhaled, letting out a long, slow breath. "It's the very best thing in the world. You make me so happy." He pressed his lips to mine, his kiss slow and sweet.

"You make me happy too," I murmured when he pulled back.

"Good."

"Are you going to tell me why you sent me out all afternoon and why the office is deserted?"

"I wanted you alone."

"We could have gone home and been alone."

"No, I wanted you alone here." He gestured to the wide expanse around us. "You were here when this was nothing but a dream. A plan."

"A three-step one, I think." I grinned.

"Yep. I've been working on another one."

"I see. Care to fill me in?"

Still holding my hand, he turned back to the railing. "I had another working model hung. Tell me what you think. Personally, I think it is my best work ever."

I looked at the various models, trying to find the new one and wondering where it came from. I knew all of them, their placement, and the history of each. I squinted and Mitch chuckled.

"Let me flip on the light," he said, pushing the button on the column.

It only took me a moment to locate a new addition. It was almost right in front of me, but so small, I hadn't noticed it right away. But once the light hit it, it was impossible not to see it—or to gasp.

Brilliant glimmers of light reflected all around me, radiating from the small box. My hand flew to my mouth, and I tried to hold back my shock. Mitch eased closer, his voice raspy.

"It's my greatest three-step plan ever, don't you think, Mandy?" He smiled. "I got you to fall in love with me, move in with me, and the final step is the rest of your life—spent with me."

I stared at him through my tears. He leaned past me, easily plucking the ring from the tiny shelf it rested on. He sank to one knee, holding out the ring.

"Please," he said quietly. "Be my wife."

Four small words, said with so much love and humility, there was only one possible answer.

"Yes."

He slid the ring onto my finger and kissed it. I stared at the three, large, round diamonds, the gems perfect and clear. I flexed my fingers, the ring feeling heavy and strange, but right on my hand. I met his tender gaze.

"Three for all our steps, Mandy—past, present, and future. All equally the same size, because they are all equally important. Our past is what made us, *us*. Our present is what makes our life so amazing, and our future is bright, because we'll be together."

He slid his fingers under my chin and kissed me. His love and devotion filled that kiss.

"That's why you got me out of the office," I whispered. "To hang the ring?"

"Well that, and I needed supplies for tonight."

"Tonight?"

He smiled—the wide, mischievous one that made his eyes crinkle—and his dimples popped. It was my favorite smile.

"Yeah, I invited a few people to celebrate with us."

"Oh?"

He leaned over the railing and yelled.

"She said yes!"

The lights came on, and I gasped as I saw his family and our friends below us on the next level down. Someone released balloons, and they shot into the air, balls of blue, green, white, and gold filling the center space and making me laugh. He had done this. Arranged it.

I glanced at him. "What if I'd said no?"

He chuckled, pressing a kiss to the side of my mouth. "They would have stayed silent and let us leave. But I was pretty certain of your answer." He met my gaze. "You don't mind I invited them to join us, do you?"

I met his eyes and shook my head. "No." I glanced down at my slacks and sweater. "I'm not dressed for a party, though."

His eyes danced. "I took care of that."

"The packages," I guessed.

He grinned. "Yep. Everything is there. Go pick what you want to wear. I'll wait, and then we'll join our guests. Everything is laid out downstairs."

"I love you," I whispered.

He tugged me close. "I love you, Mandy." He lifted my hand and kissed my ring again. "And now it's official. I get to keep you."

"And I get to keep you."

"Forever. No exchanges, no refunds."

"I can live with that."

He yanked me close, his voice suddenly serious. "Soon, sweetheart? You'll marry me soon?"

"If that's what you want."

"It's exactly what I want. I want to marry you and take you on a honeymoon."

"That works for me."

"I was thinking a clothing-optional honeymoon. And by optional, I mean none. You, me, a private place, and all the sex we can manage."

Smiling, I traced his face with my fingers. "Knowing you—that's a lot of sex."

"Count on it."

I looked down at the small gathering below us. Music was already playing, and I heard the sounds of drinks being made, the laughter of our friends, and I knew whatever he had planned would be amazing.

"This—" I swallowed, emotions beginning to overwhelm me "—this is more than I ever expected. You're more than I ever expected." A giggle burst through my lips. "I was planning on seducing you with a cupcake and a blowjob to get you to open up to me tonight."

He threw back his head in laughter and kissed me again. This time, his lips were hungry, his touch possessive, and his tongue wicked. He drew back, his breathing hard.

"Hold on to that thought, sweetheart. I'll take you up on that later." He lifted his chin with a smile, nudging me away. "Now go and get ready before I change my mind and fuck you senseless before the party."

I walked away, looking over my shoulder with a wink. "You know—they have booze. Another ten minutes won't hurt anyone."

He jerked, unsure of what to do. Walking backward, I solved his problem by peeling my sweater over my head, showing him the lacy black lingerie underneath it. I slid my finger under the waistband of my pants.

"They match. Wanna see?"

He rushed toward me, shrugging off his jacket and yanking on his tie. With a laugh, I hurried toward his office, knowing he would follow.

He shut his door, watching me with hooded eyes. "Ten minutes might end up being fifteen."

I dropped my pants, letting him see the skimpy, barely there underwear. He licked his lips, grappling with his belt.

"Or twenty."

I lowered myself to my knees and whistled softly.

He groaned, then shook his head.

"Fuck it. It's an open bar."

I laughed and he leaned down, kissing my mouth.

"And we have cupcakes."

I met his lust-filled gaze.

"Perfect."

ACKNOWLEDGMENTS

Thank you to Tessa Bailey and Alexa Riley for asking me to be part of Read Me Romance. It was a blast to write this story.

To Deb and Lisa–many thanks for your keen eyes. Melissa and Peggy–you rock.

Many thanks to my beta readers, my reading group Melanie's Minions, my review team, and to all the bloggers and reviewers. Your support means so much.

Karen—thank you for all your efforts. I know at times you wonder how I function without your guidance—but hey—what job security! Love you bunches!

To my lovely readers—you are the reason I do this daily. Your love, support, and encouragement means the world to me. Thank you from the bottom of my heart.

ALSO BY MELANIE MORELAND

Vested Interest Series

Bentley (Vested Interest #1)

Aiden (Vested Interest #2)

Maddox (Vested Interest #3)

Reid (Vested Interest #4)

Van (Vested Interest #5)

Halton (Vested Interest #6)

Insta-Spark Collection

It Started with a Kiss

Christmas Sugar

An Instant Connection

The Contract Series

The Contract

The Baby Clause (Contract #2)

Standalones

Into the Storm

Beneath the Scars

Over the Fence

My Image of You (Random House/Loveswept)

New York Times/USA Today bestselling author Melanie Moreland, lives a happy and content life in a quiet area of Ontario with her beloved husband of twenty-nine-plus years and their rescue cat, Amber. Nothing means more to her than her friends and family, and she cherishes every moment spent with them.

While seriously addicted to coffee, and highly challenged with all things computer-related and technical, she relishes baking, cooking, and trying new recipes for people to sample. She loves to throw dinner parties, and enjoys travelling, here and abroad, but finds coming home is always the best part of any trip.

Melanie loves stories, especially paired with a good wine, and enjoys skydiving (free falling over a fleck of dust) extreme snowboarding (falling down stairs) and piloting her own helicopter (tripping over her own feet). She's learned happily ever afters, even bumpy ones, are all in how you tell the story.

Melanie is represented by Flavia Viotti at Bookcase Literary Agency. For any questions regarding subsidiary or translation rights please contact her at flavia@bookcaseagency.com

Connect with Melanie

Like reader groups? Lots of fun and giveaways! Check it out Melanie Moreland's Minions

Join my newsletter for up-to-date news, sales, book announcements and excerpts (no spam): Melanie Moreland's newsletter

Visit my website www.melaniemoreland.com